SCURVY DOGS

Kevin Frank

Kane Miller
A DIVISION OF EDC PUBLISHING

Kane Miller, A Division of EDC Publishing

Text and illustrations copyright © Kevin Frank 2016

For information contact:
Kane Miller, A Division of EDC Publishing
PO Box 470663
Tulsa, OK 74147-0663
www.kanemiller.com
www.edcpub.com
www.usbornebooksandmore.com

Library of Congress Control Number: 2015954246

Manufactured by Regent Publishing Services, Hong Kong
Printed June 2016 in ShenZhen, Guangdong, China
2 3 4 5 6 7 8 9 10

ISBN: 978-1-61067-459-1

For my Scurvy Family

Chapter One

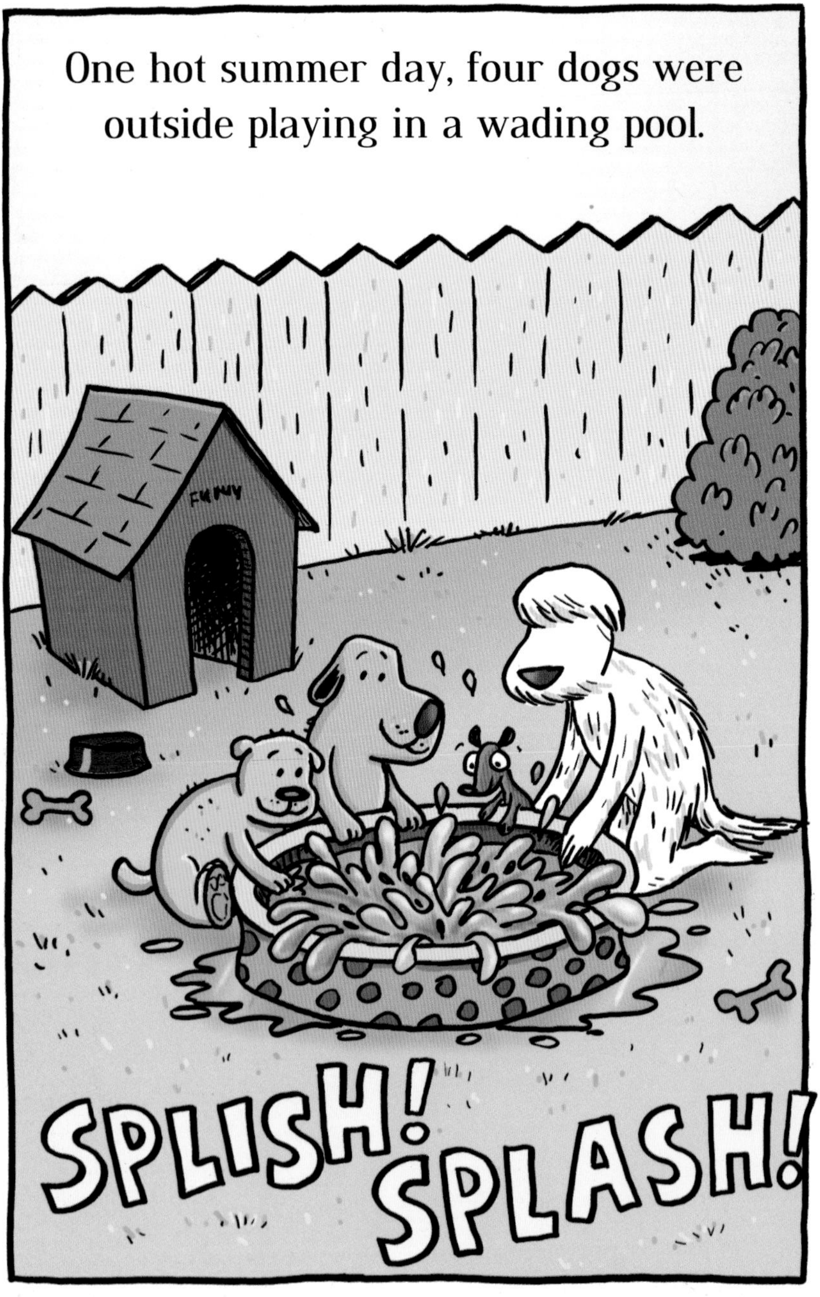
One hot summer day, four dogs were outside playing in a wading pool.
SPLISH! SPLASH!

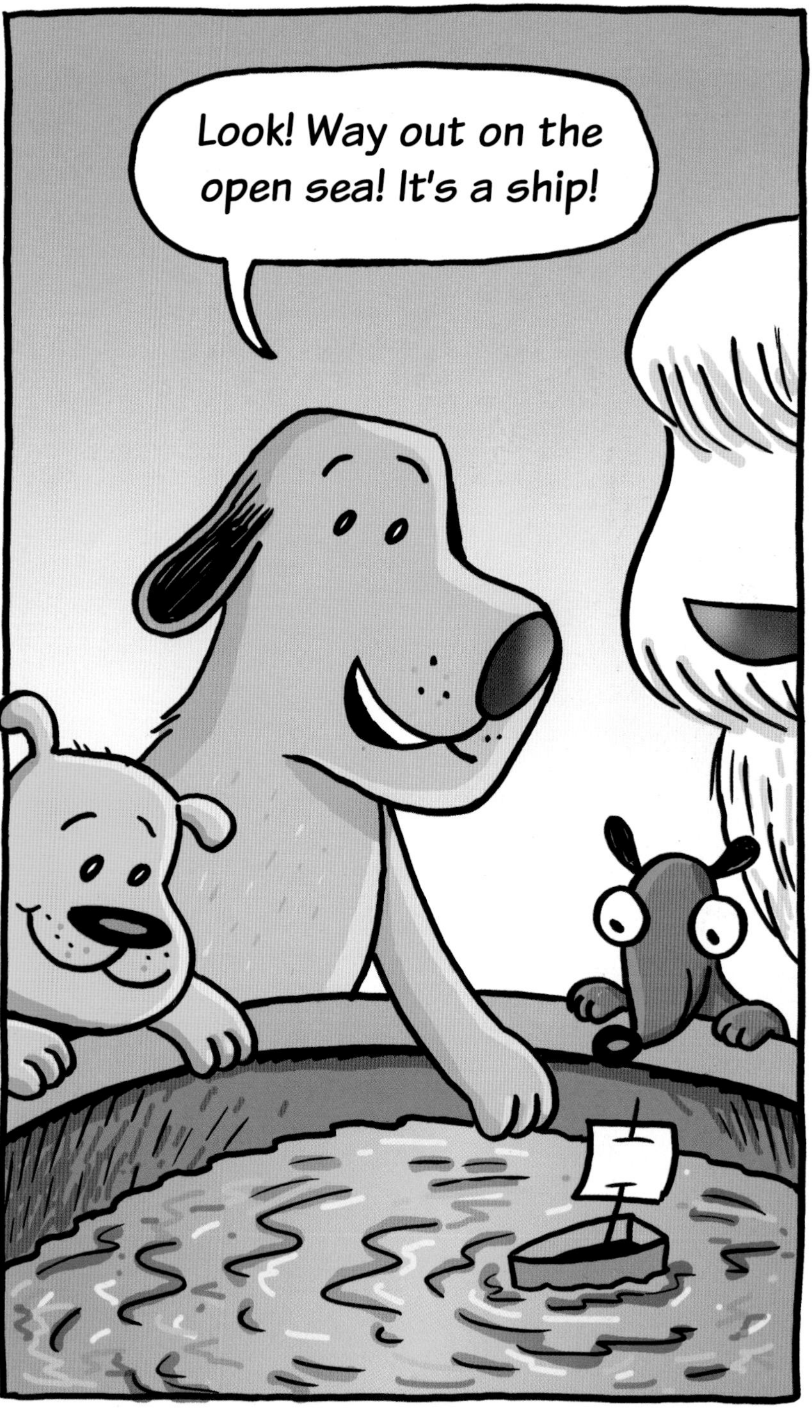
Look! Way out on the open sea! It's a ship!

And not just any ship, but a pirate ship.

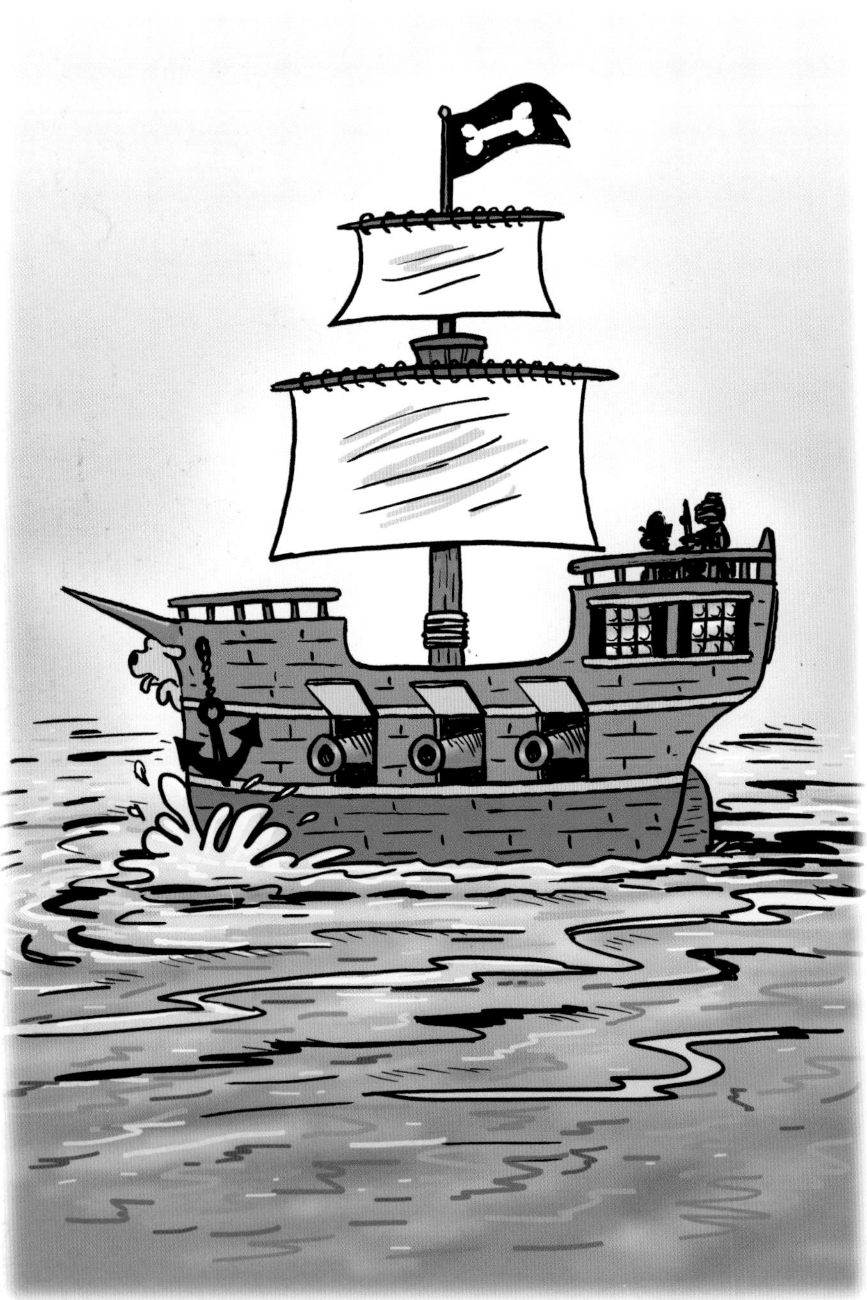

A pirate ship, crewed by a fearsome group of Scurvy Dogs:

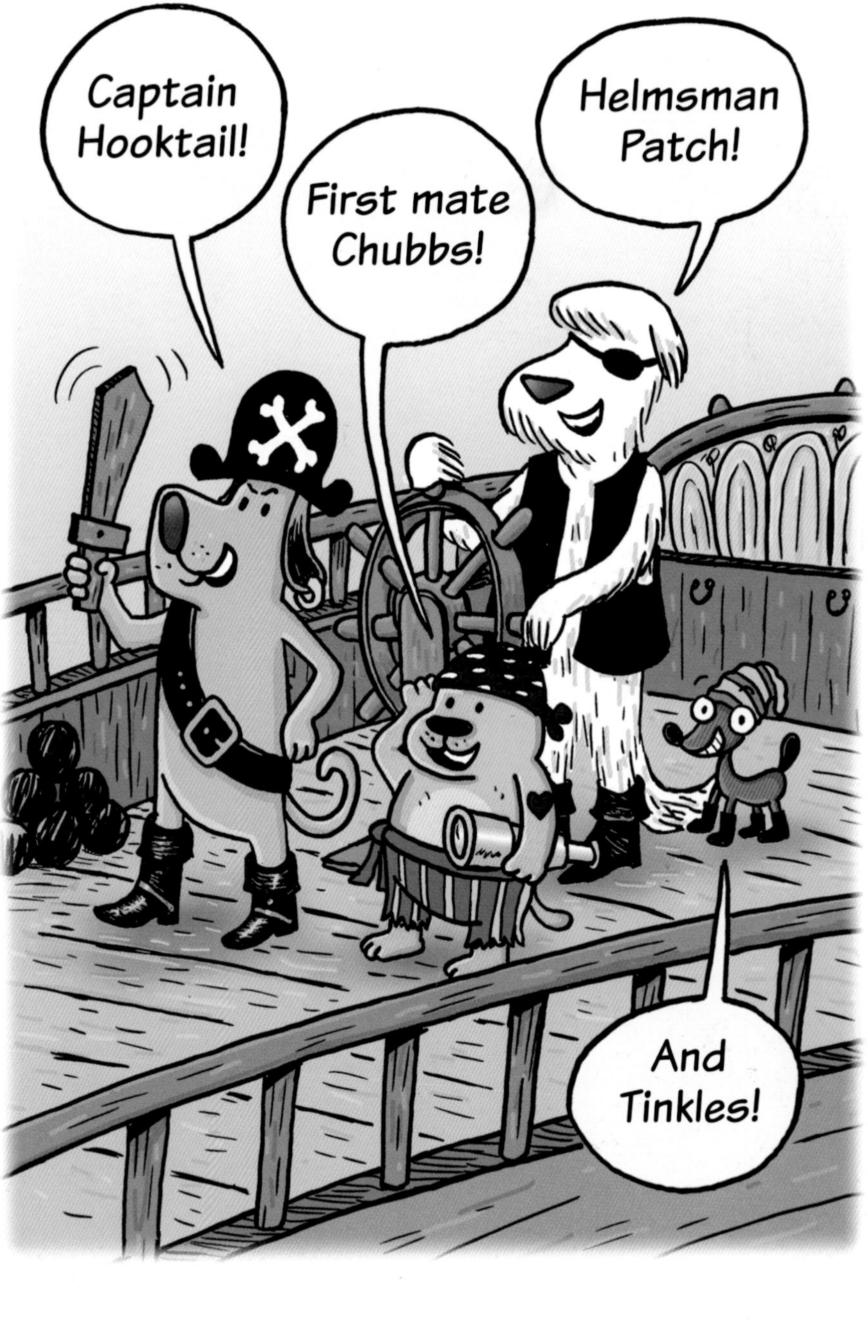

Captain Hooktail!
First mate Chubbs!
Helmsman Patch!
And Tinkles!

The pirates were celebrating because they had just sunk a ship full of their worst enemies: cats!

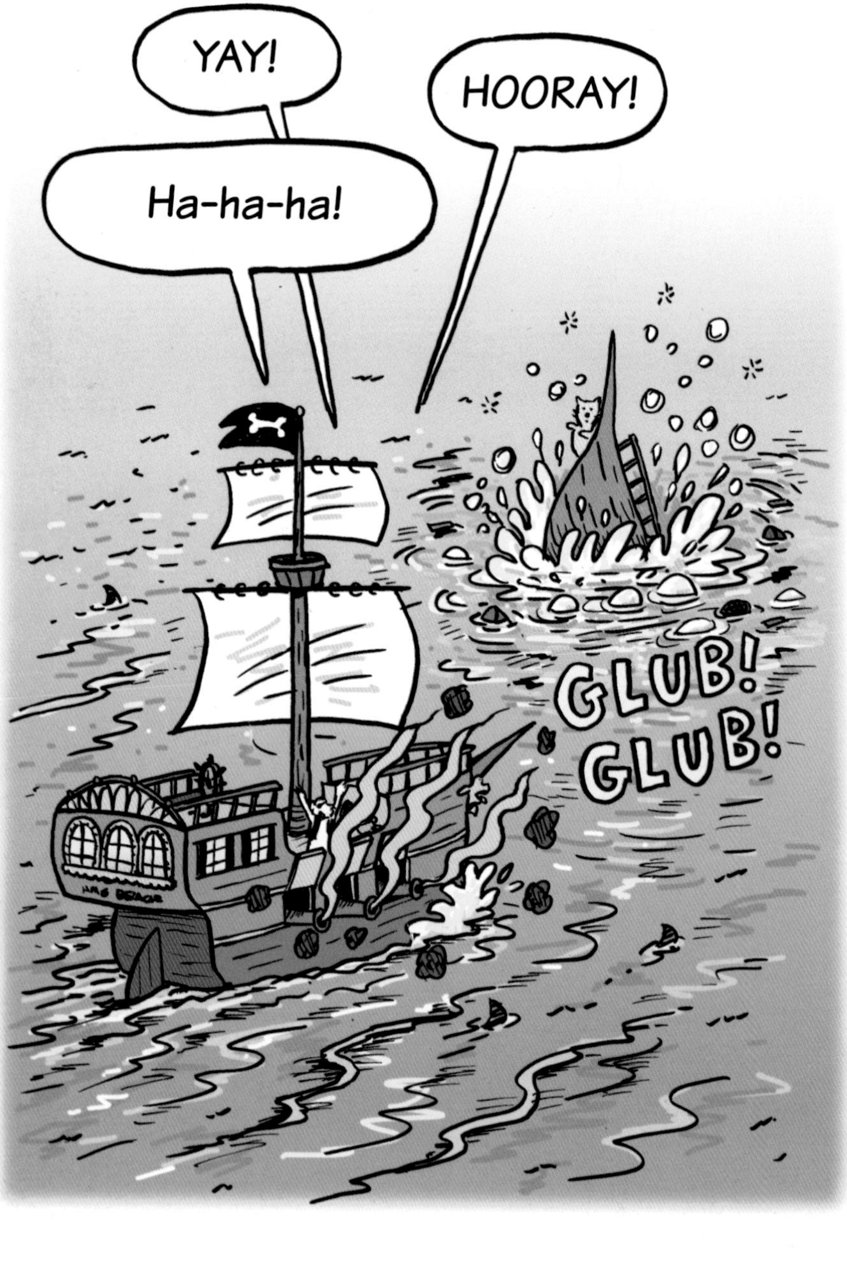
YAY!
HOORAY!
Ha-ha-ha!
GLUB! GLUB!

And now it was time to enjoy the treasure.

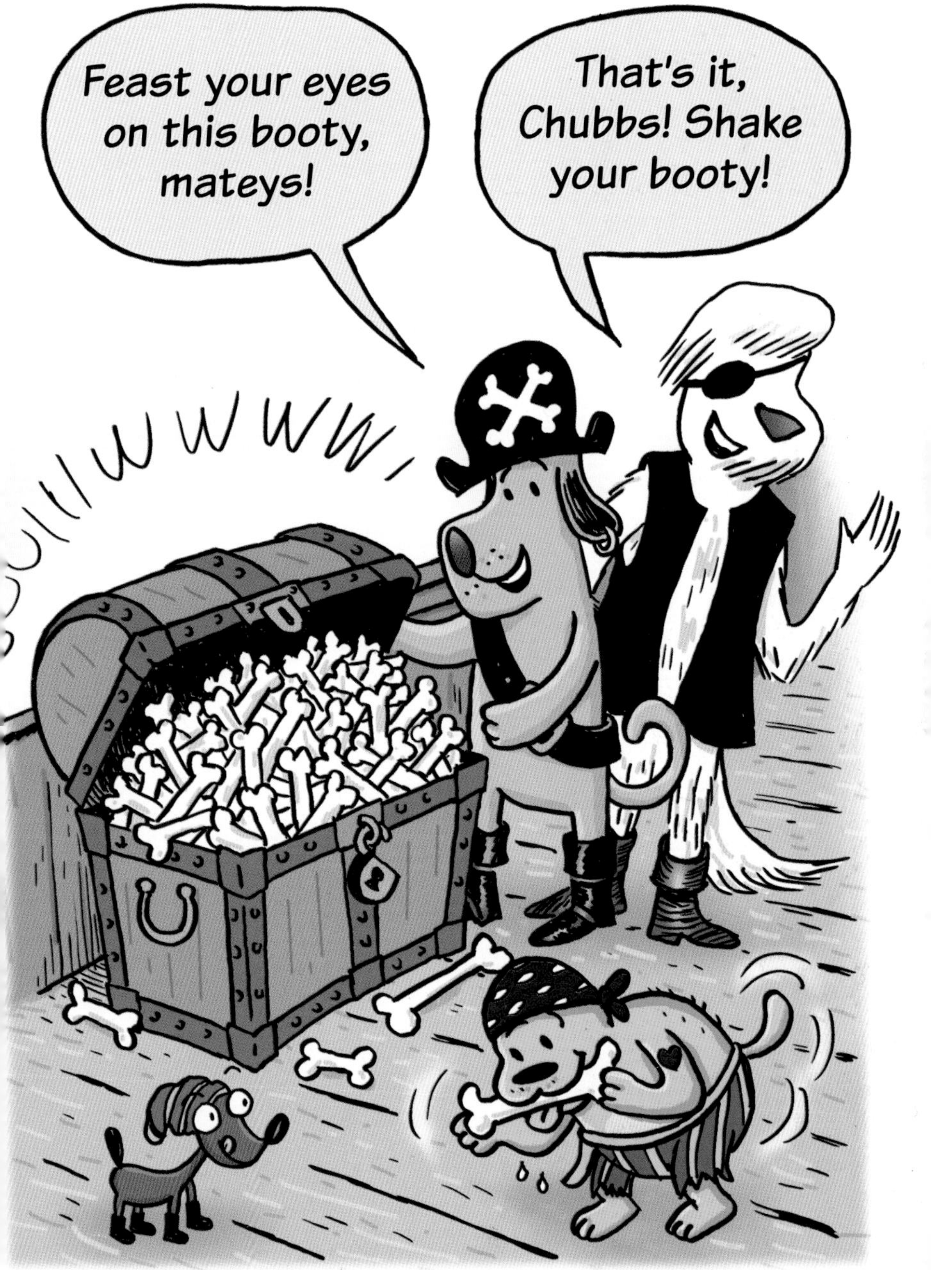
Feast your eyes on this booty, mateys!
That's it, Chubbs! Shake your booty!
WWWWW

But their enjoyment was spoiled by a horrible screeching.

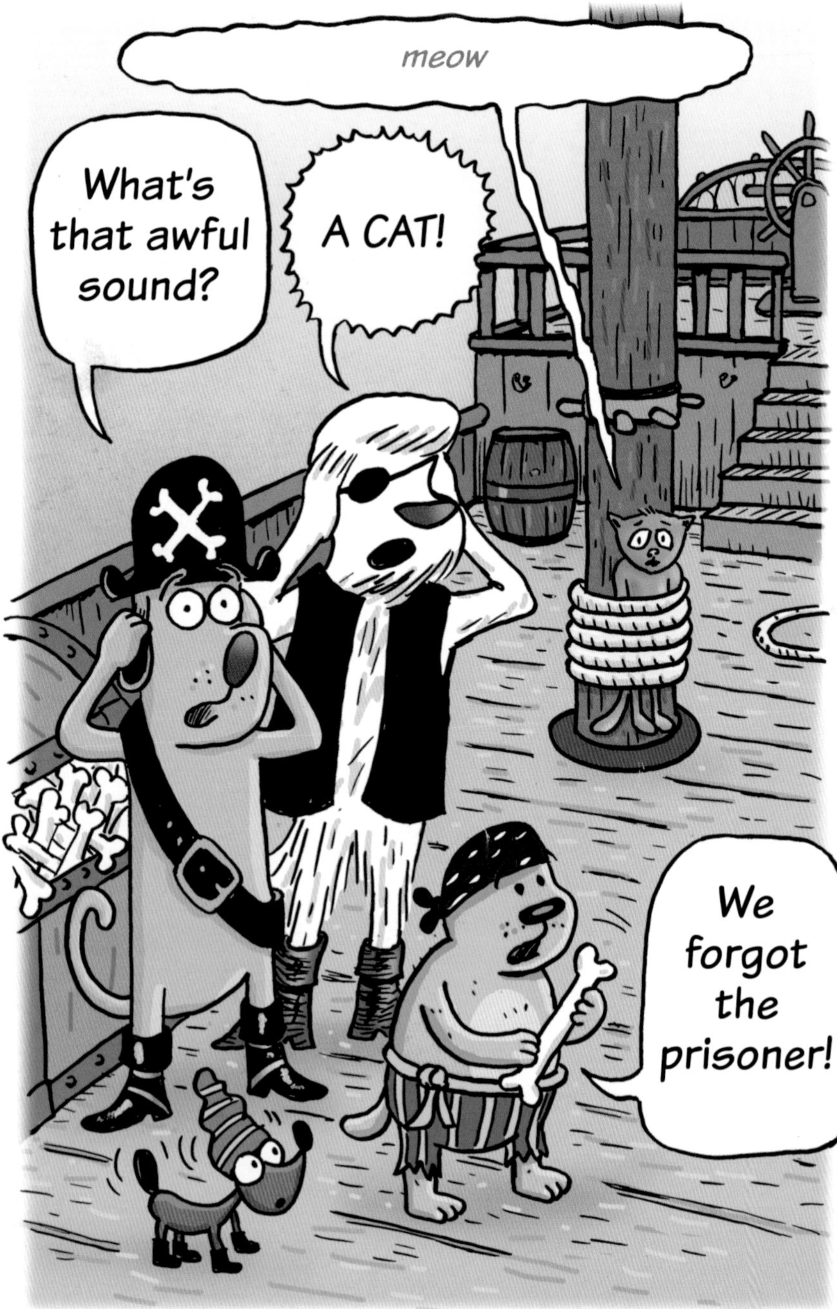
meow
What's that awful sound?
A CAT!
We forgot the prisoner!

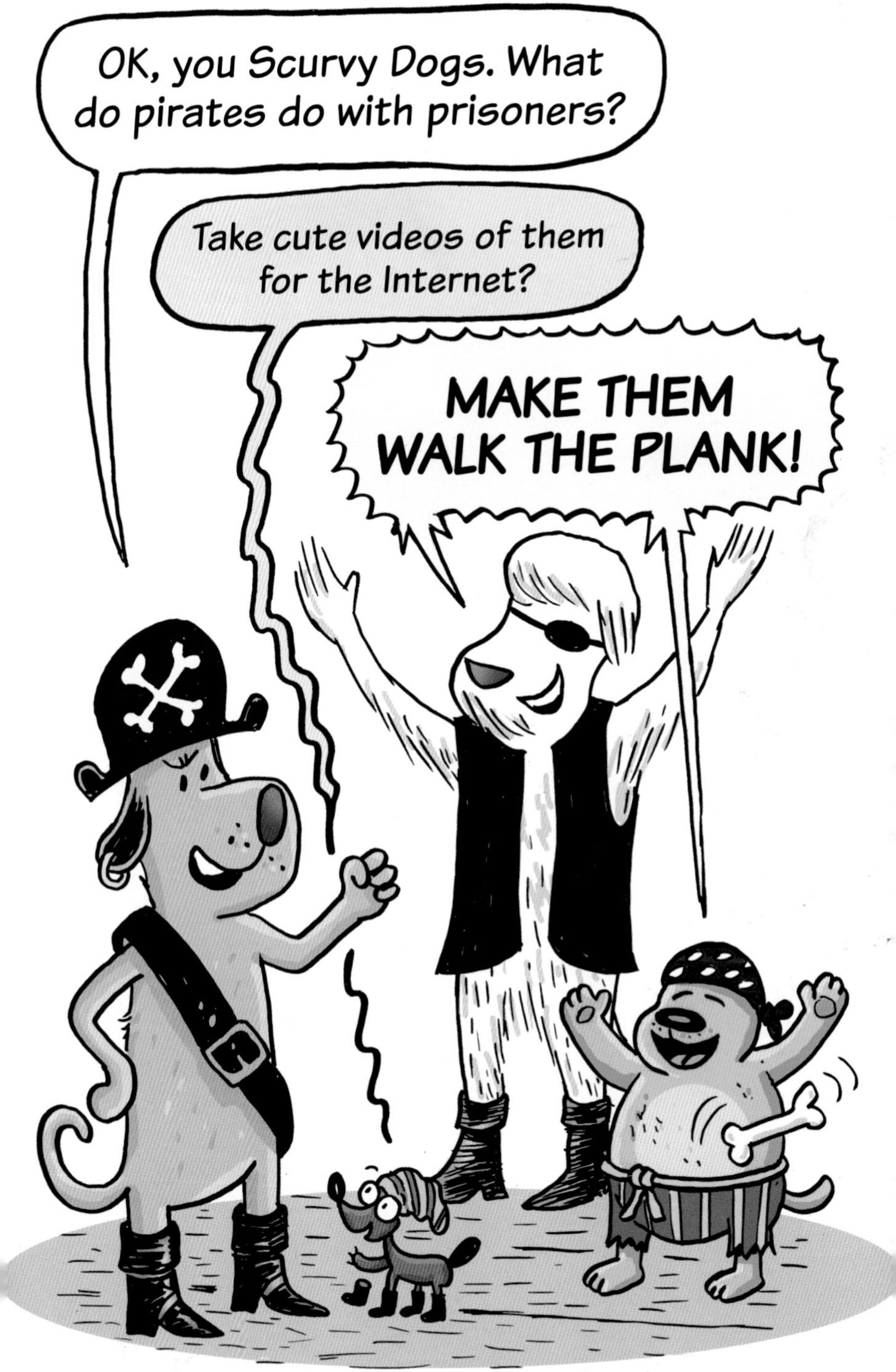
OK, you Scurvy Dogs. What do pirates do with prisoners?
Take cute videos of them for the Internet?
MAKE THEM WALK THE PLANK!

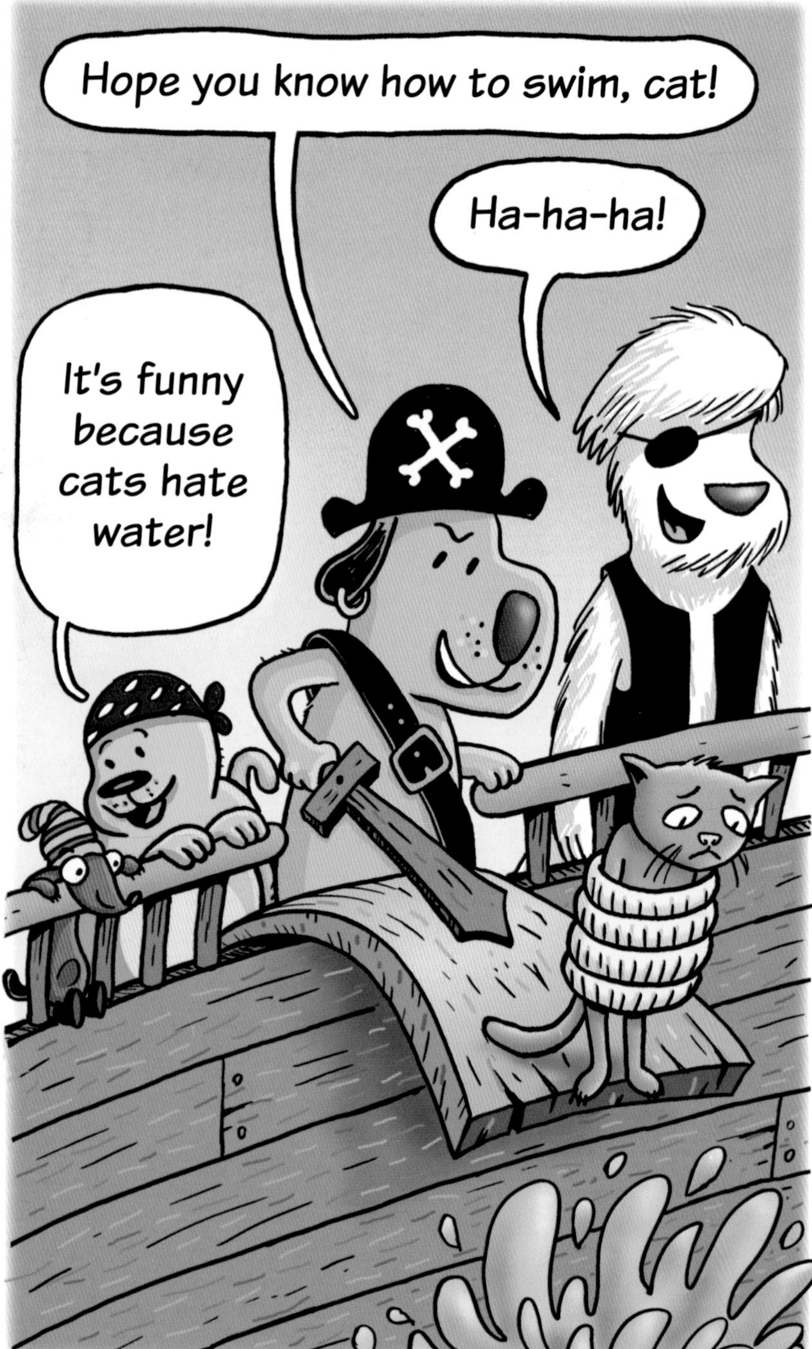
Hope you know how to swim, cat!
Ha-ha-ha!
It's funny because cats hate water!

Chapter Two

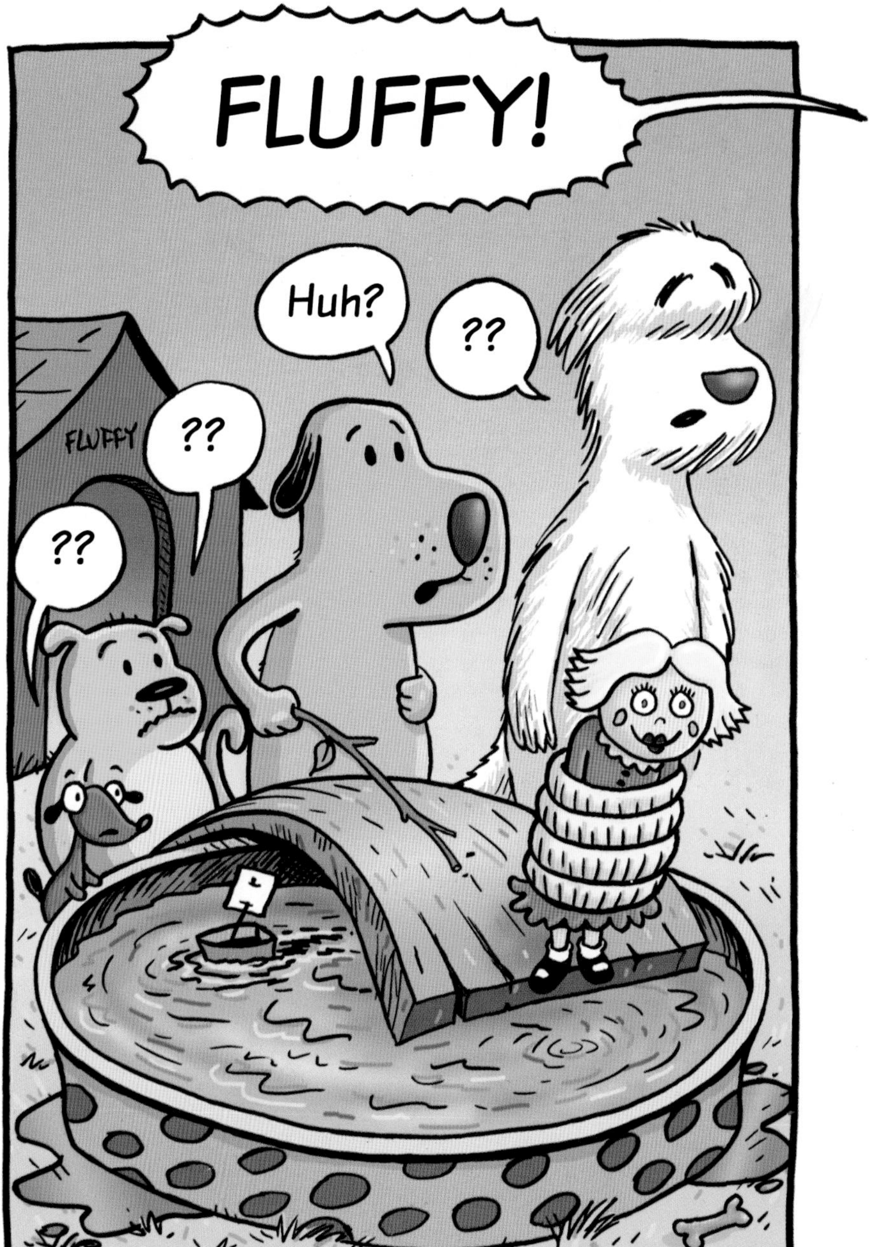
FLUFFY!
Huh?
??
??
??
FLUFFY

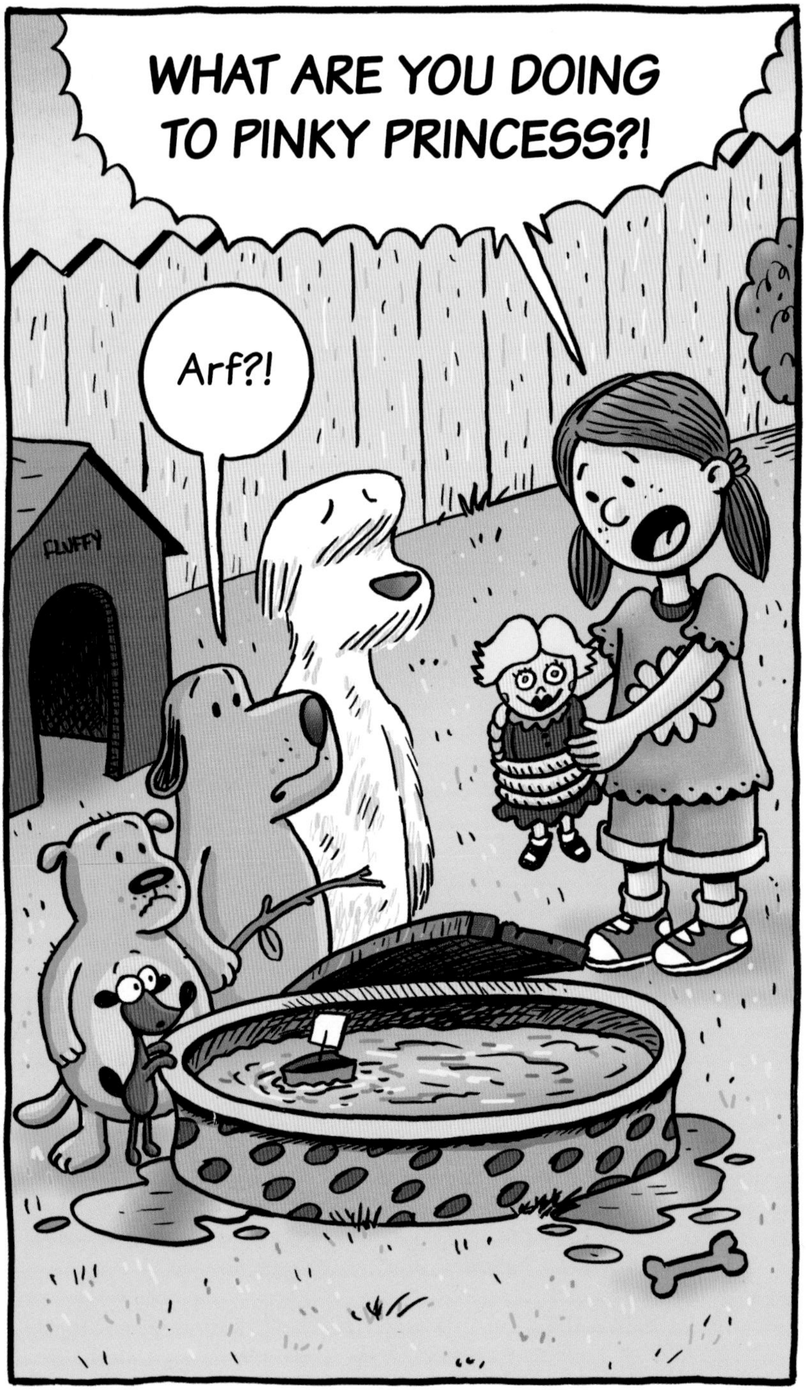
WHAT ARE YOU DOING TO PINKY PRINCESS?!
Arf?!
FLUFFY

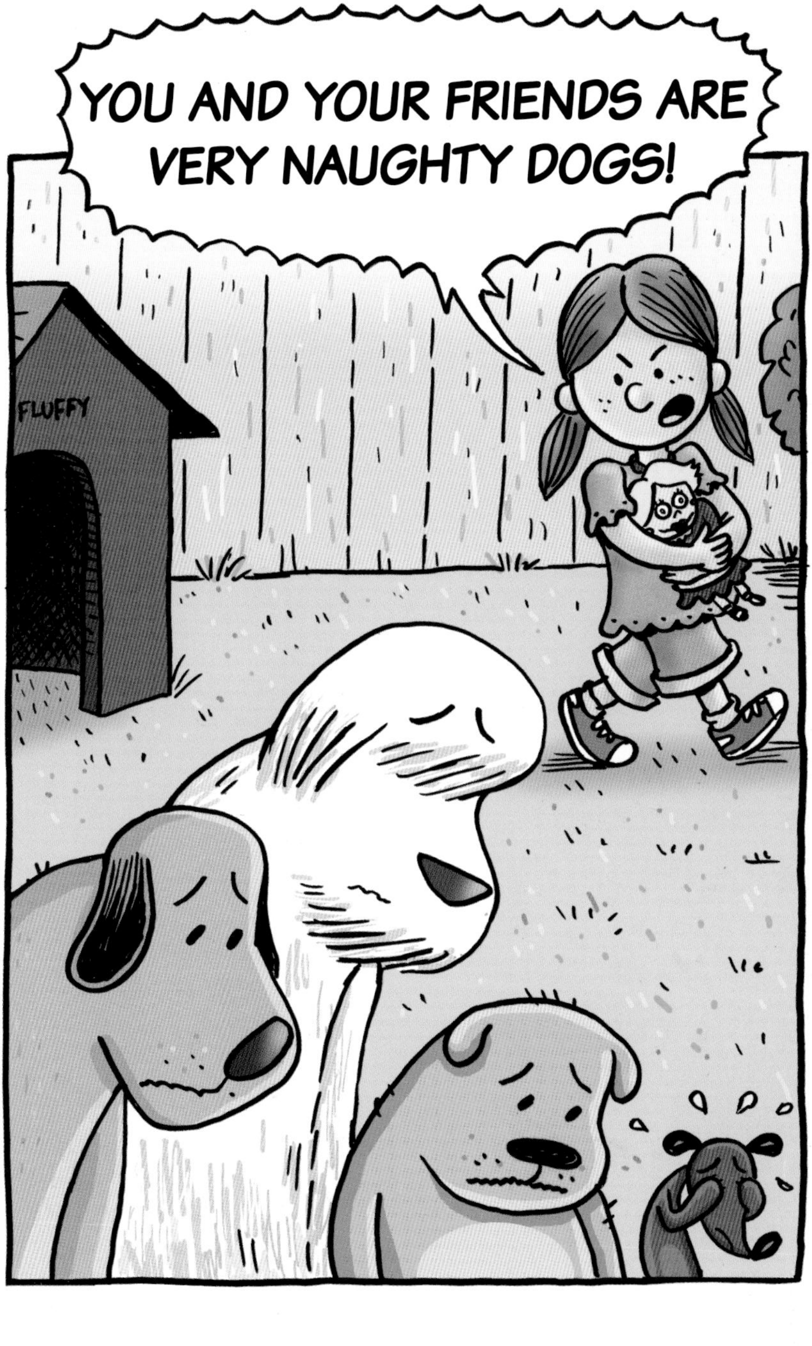
YOU AND YOUR FRIENDS ARE VERY NAUGHTY DOGS!
FLUFFY

The pirates bowed their heads in shame.

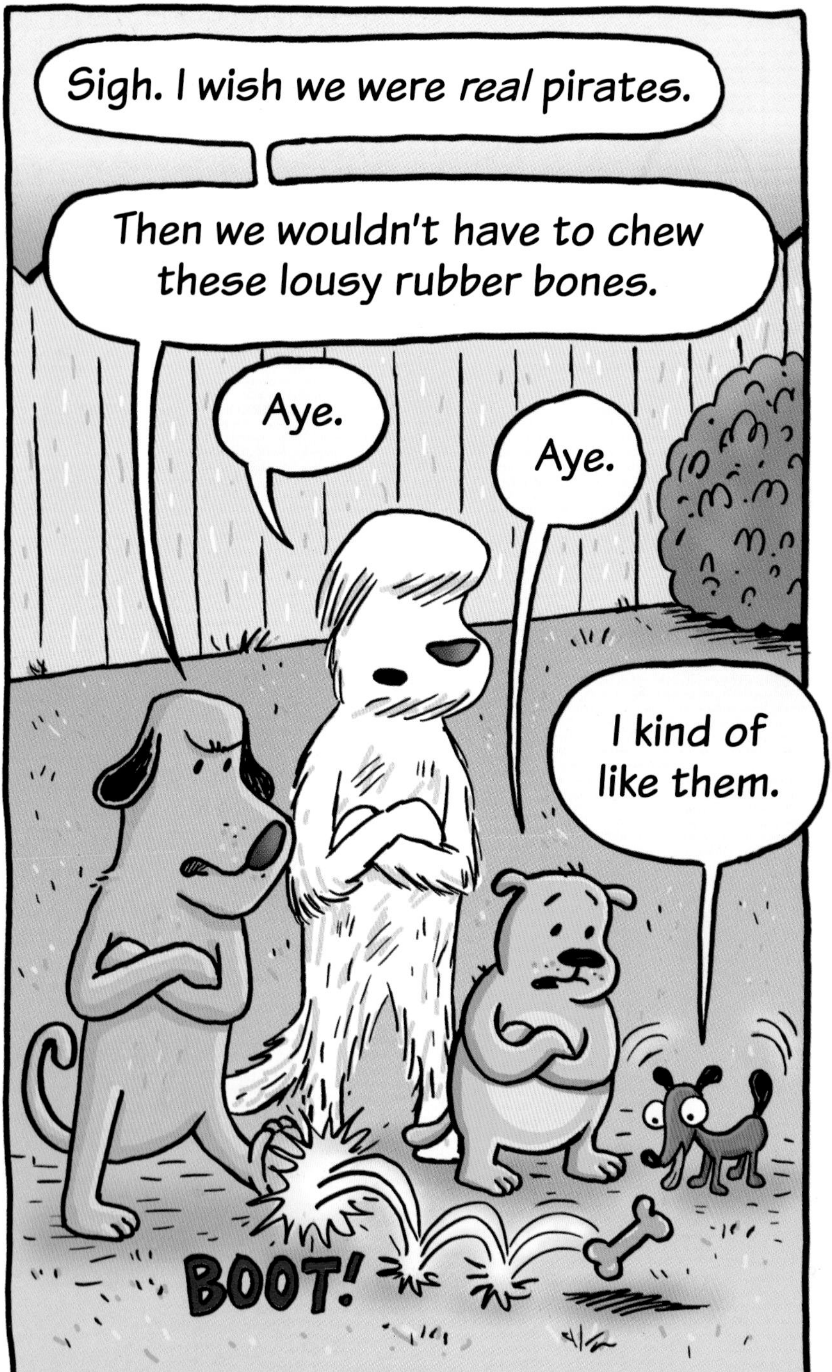
Sigh. I wish we were *real* pirates.
Then we wouldn't have to chew these lousy rubber bones.
Aye.
Aye.
I kind of like them.
BOOT!

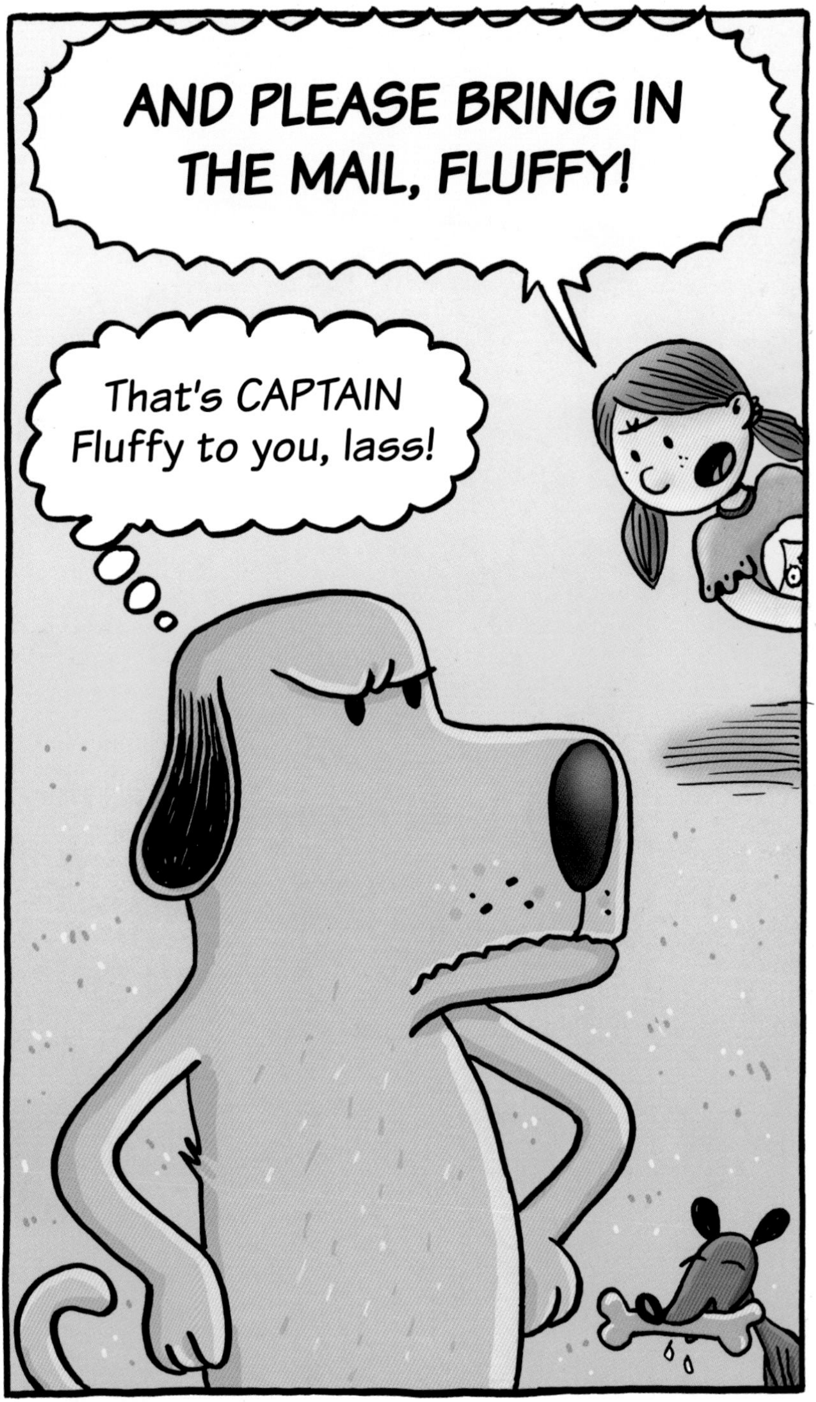
AND PLEASE BRING IN THE MAIL, FLUFFY!
That's CAPTAIN Fluffy to you, lass!

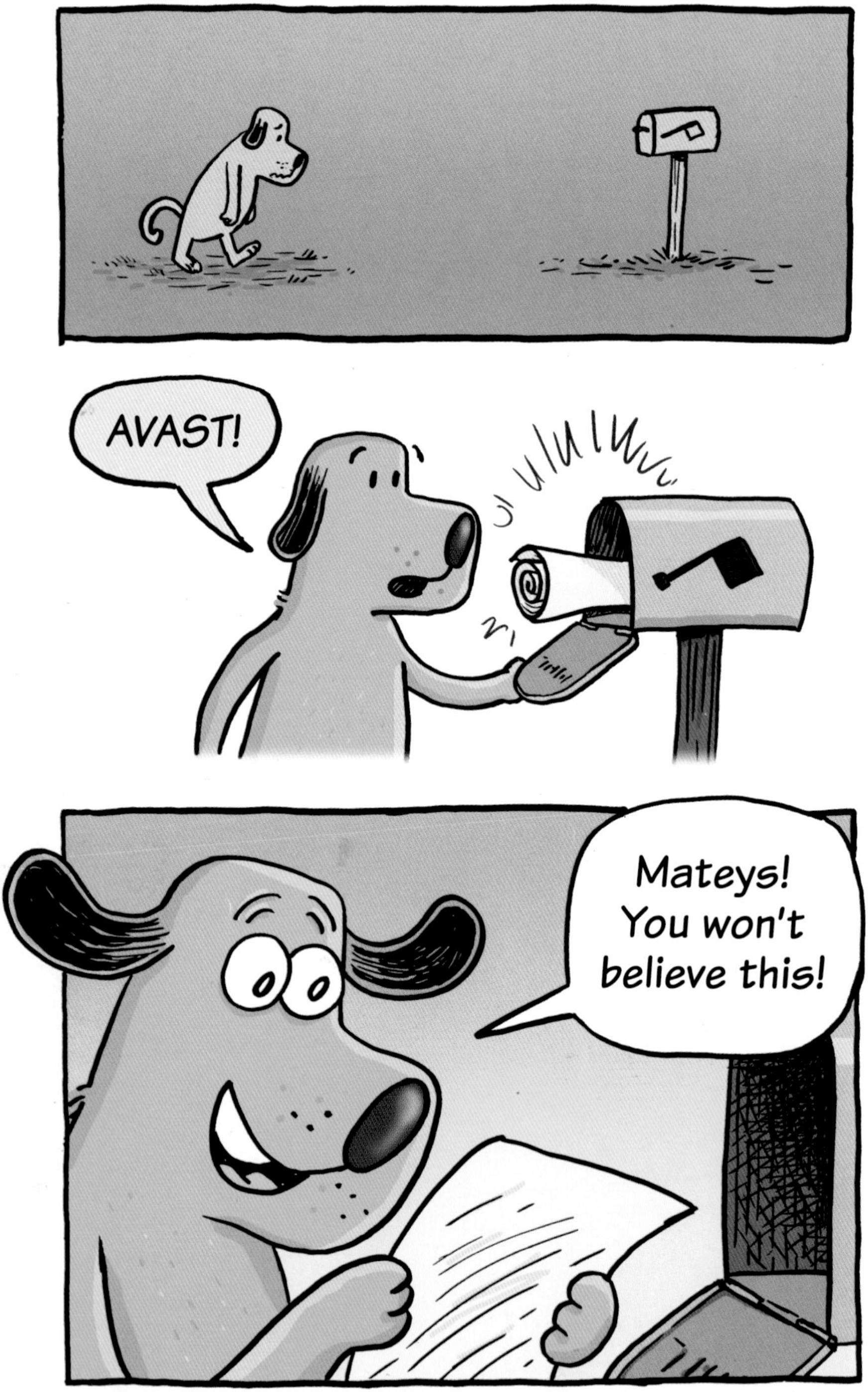
AVAST!
Mateys! You won't believe this!

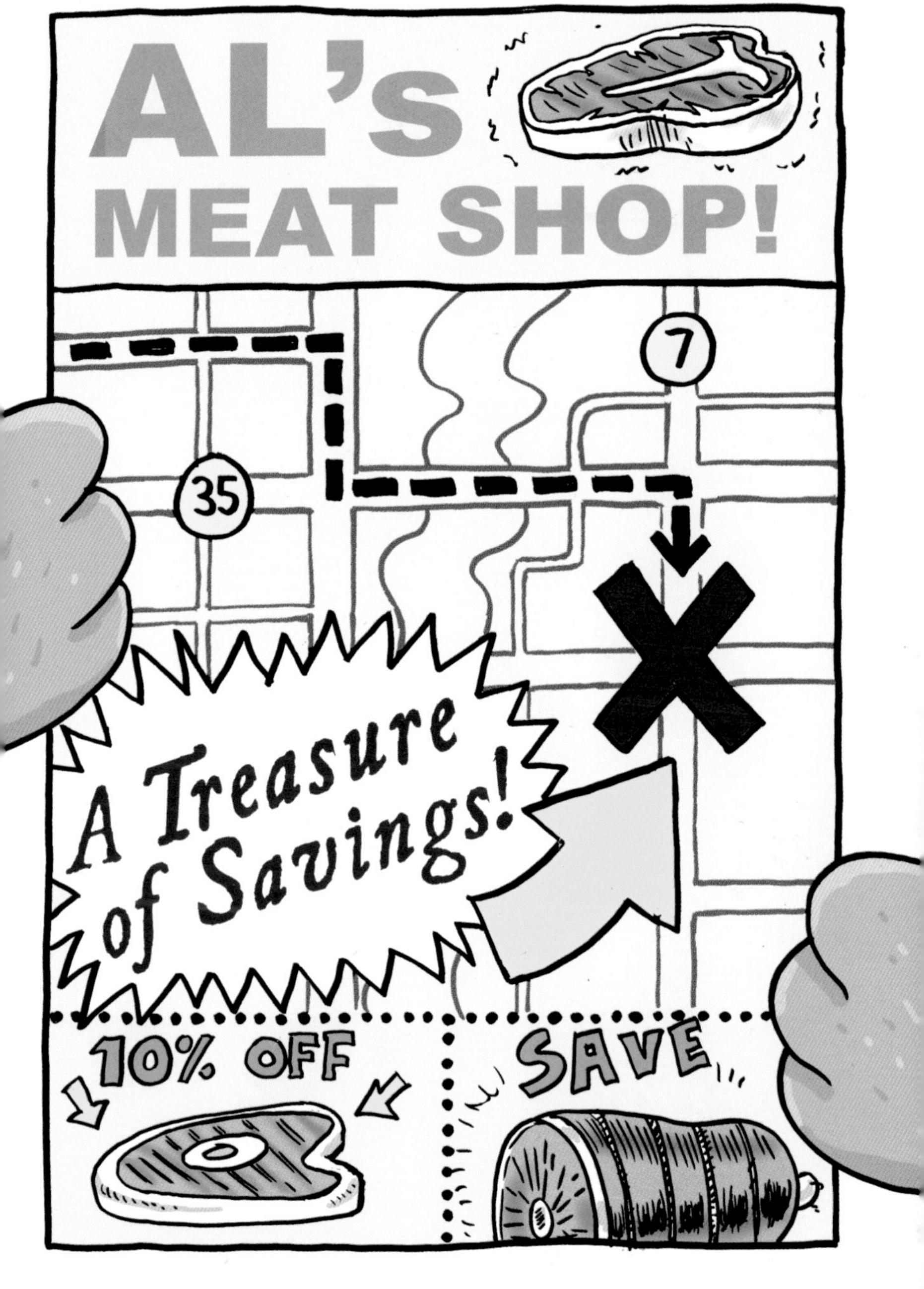
AL'S
MEAT SHOP!
7
35
A Treasure of Savings!
10% OFF
SAVE

Captain Hooktail had discovered
a treasure map!

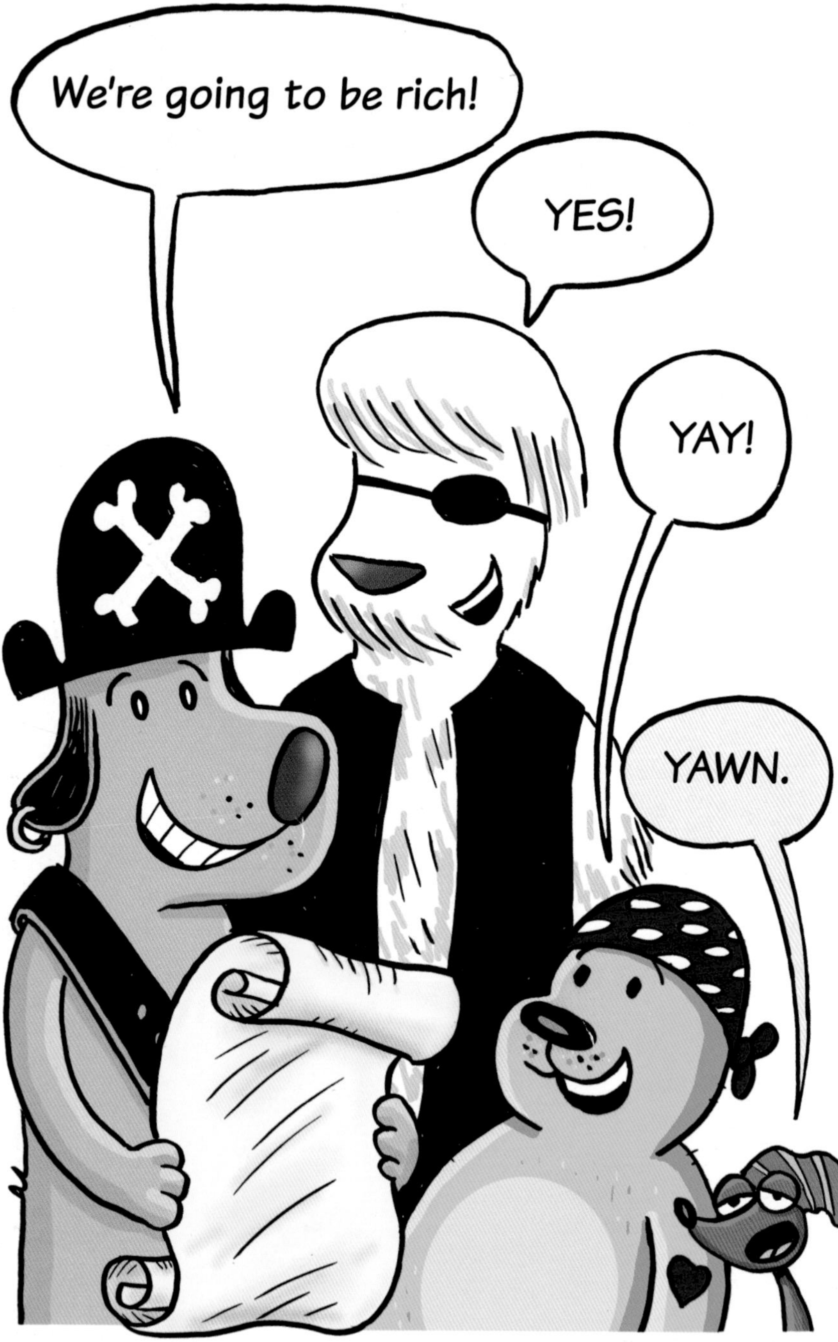
We're going to be rich!
YES!
YAY!
YAWN.

Chapter Three

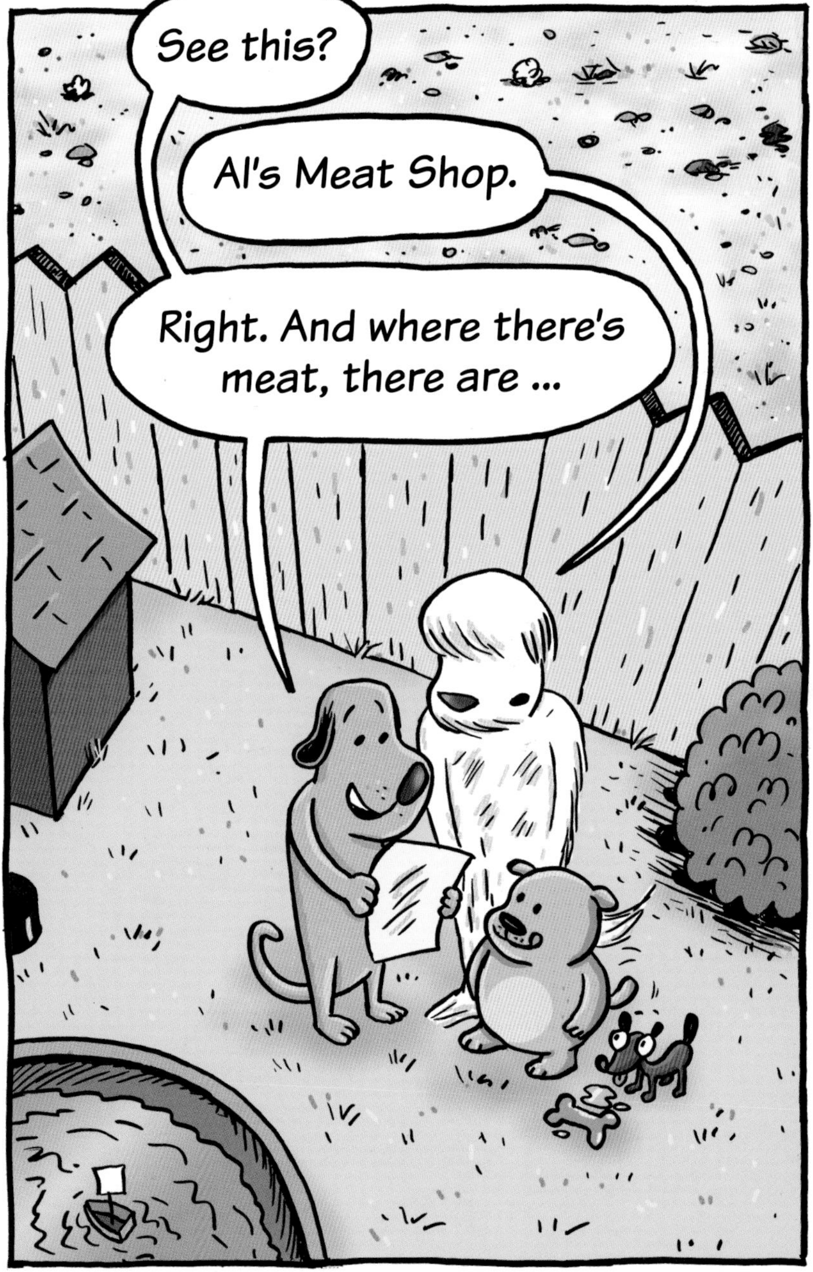

See this?
Al's Meat Shop.
Right. And where there's meat, there are ...

BONES!!!

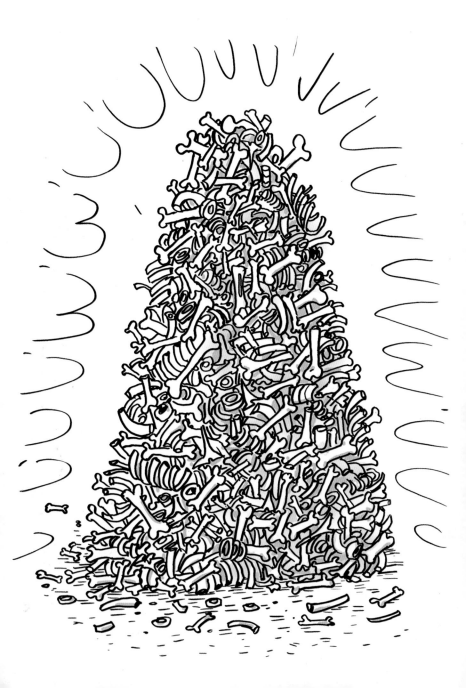

And so, the pirates decided to head for the open sea in search of treasure.

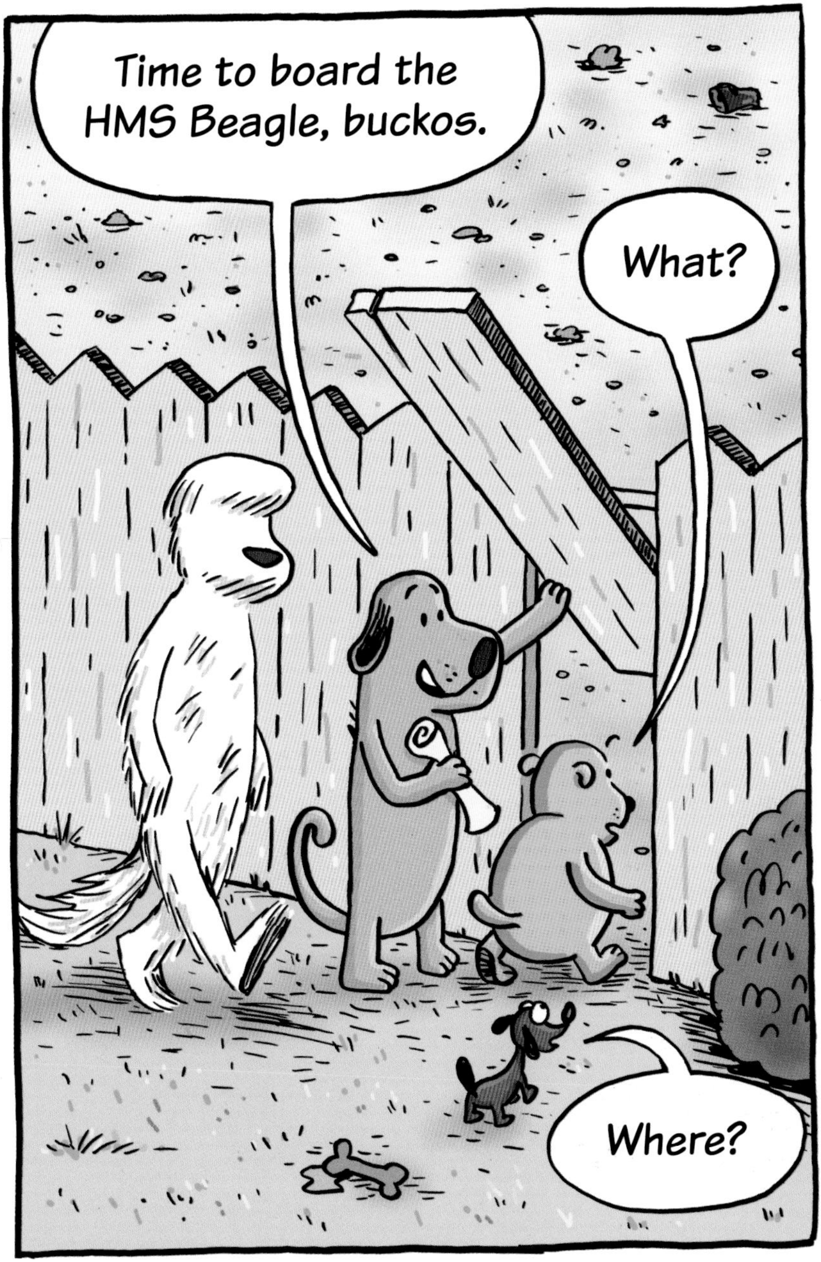
Time to board the HMS Beagle, buckos.
What?
Where?

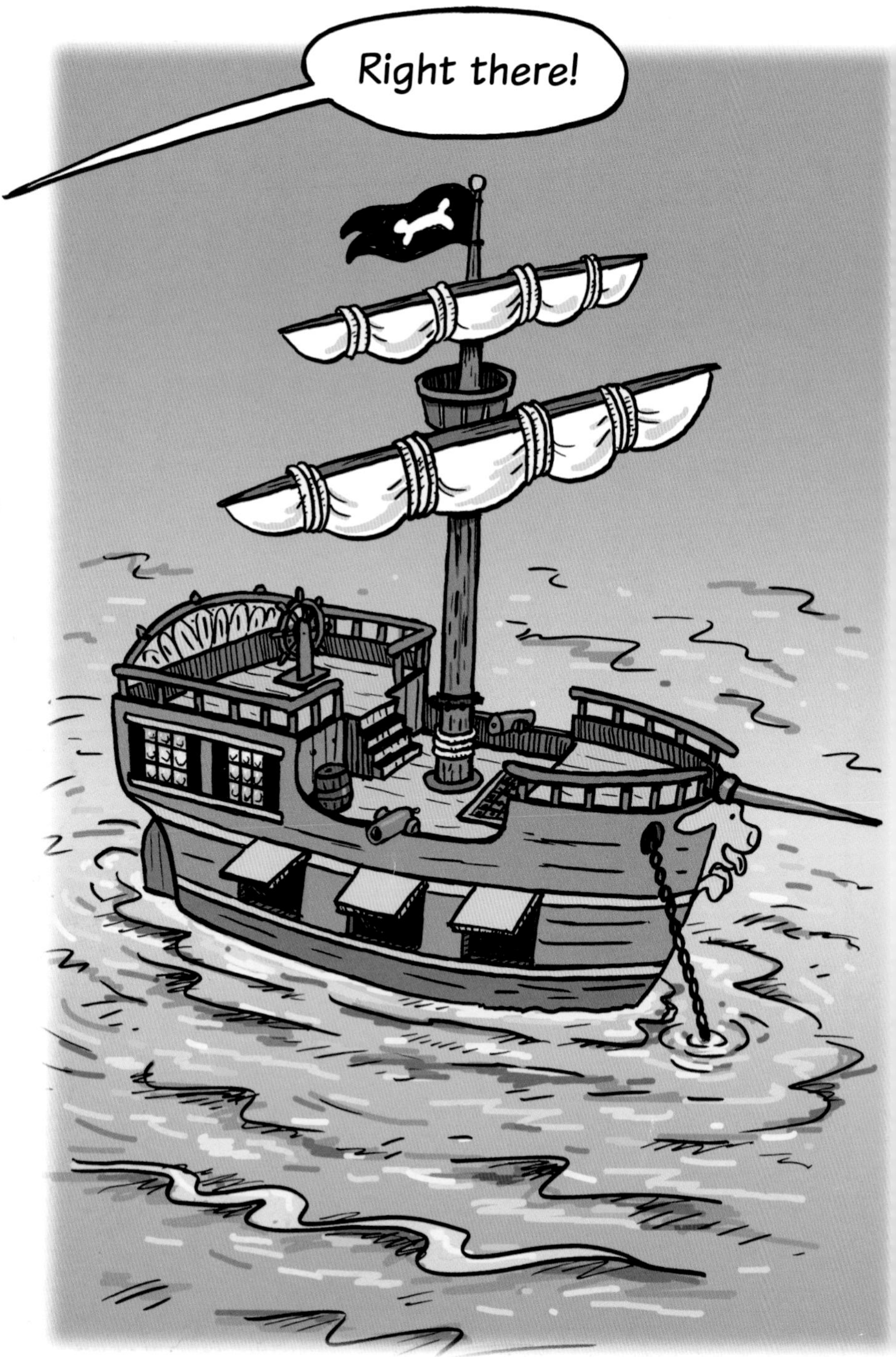
Right there!

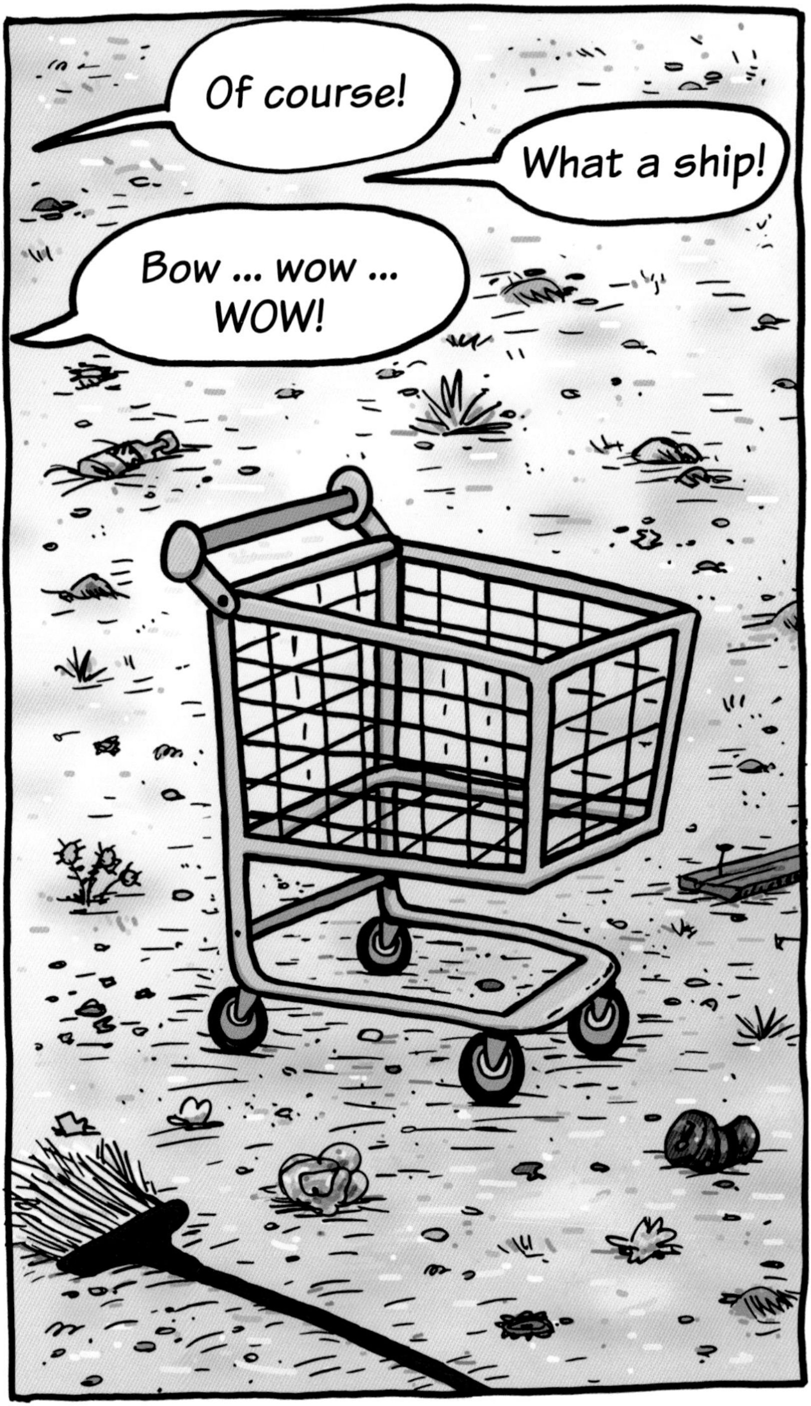
Of course!
What a ship!
Bow ... wow ...
WOW!

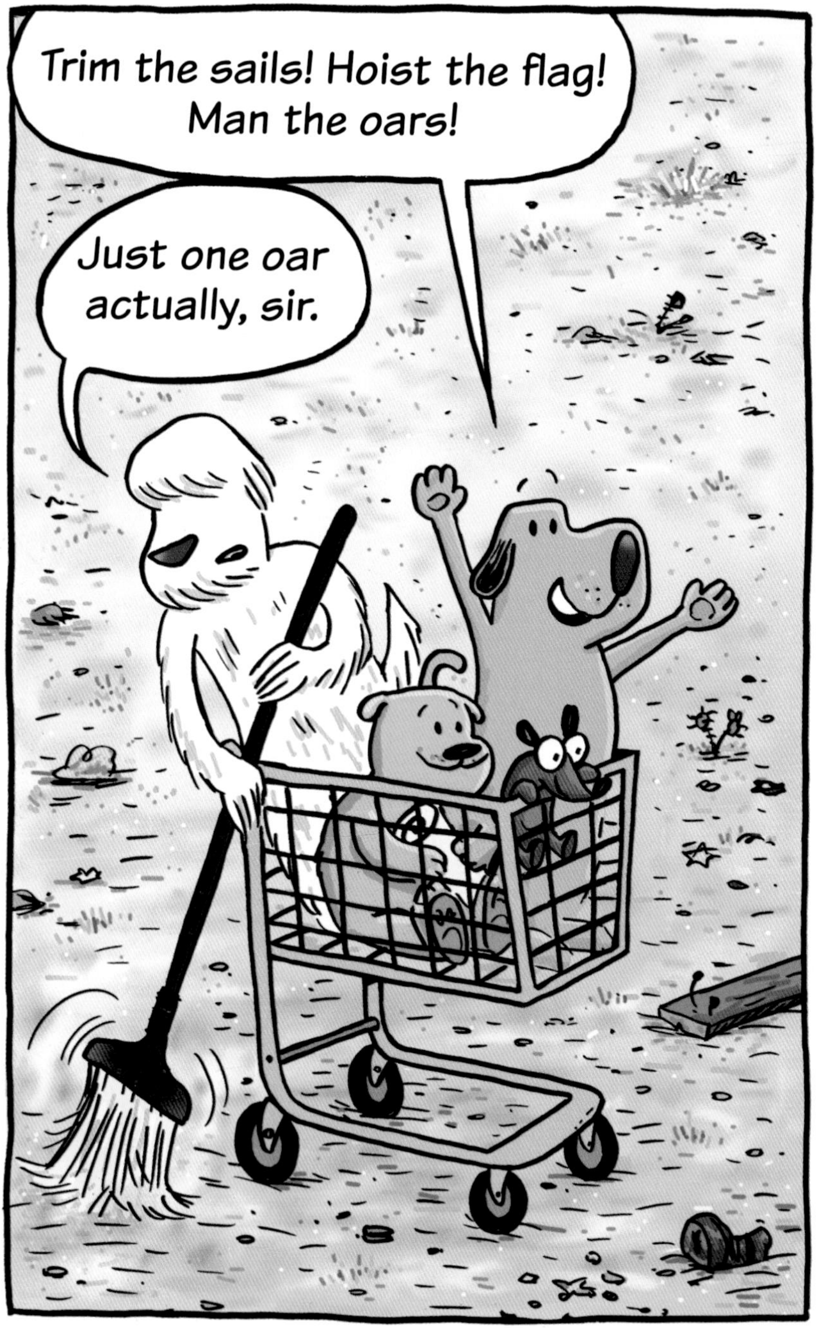
Trim the sails! Hoist the flag! Man the oars!
Just one oar actually, sir.

The Scurvy Dogs set sail.

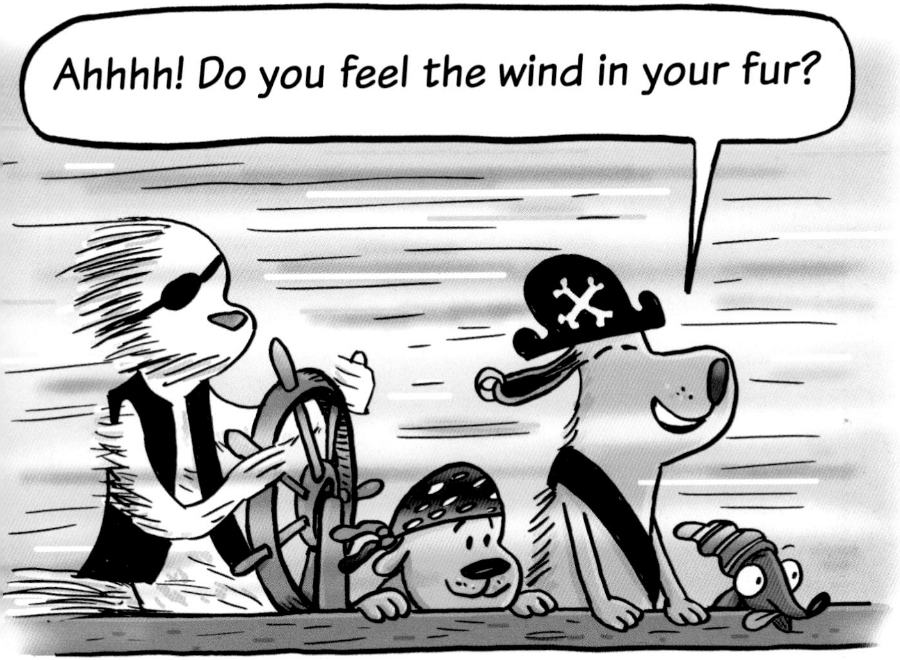
Ahhhh! Do you feel the wind in your fur?

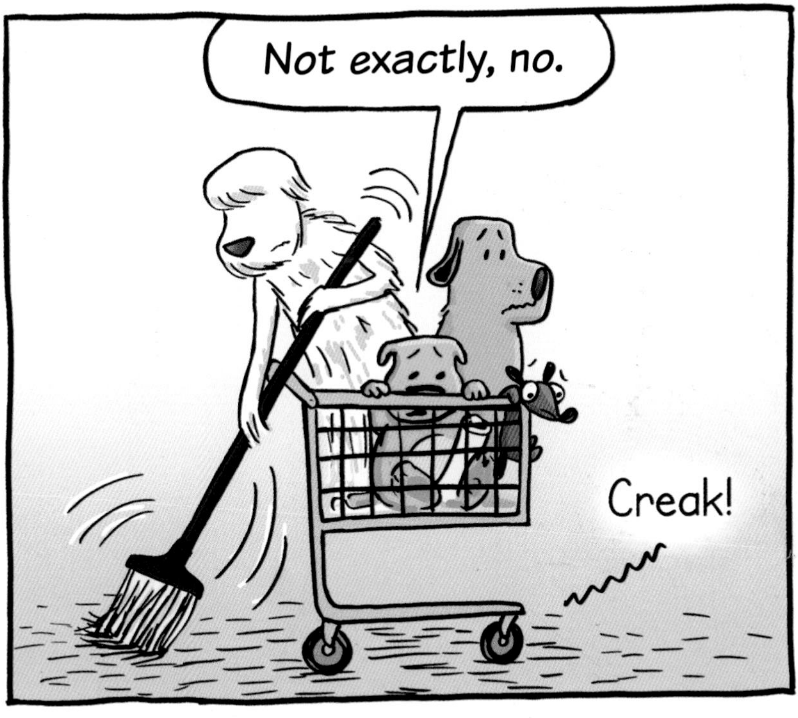
Not exactly, no.
Creak!

They moved slowly ahead.

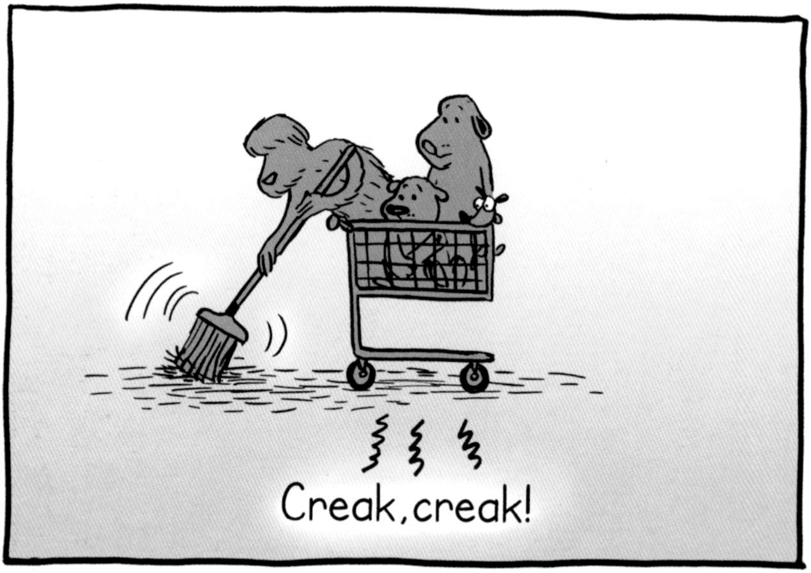
Creak, creak!

Very slowly.

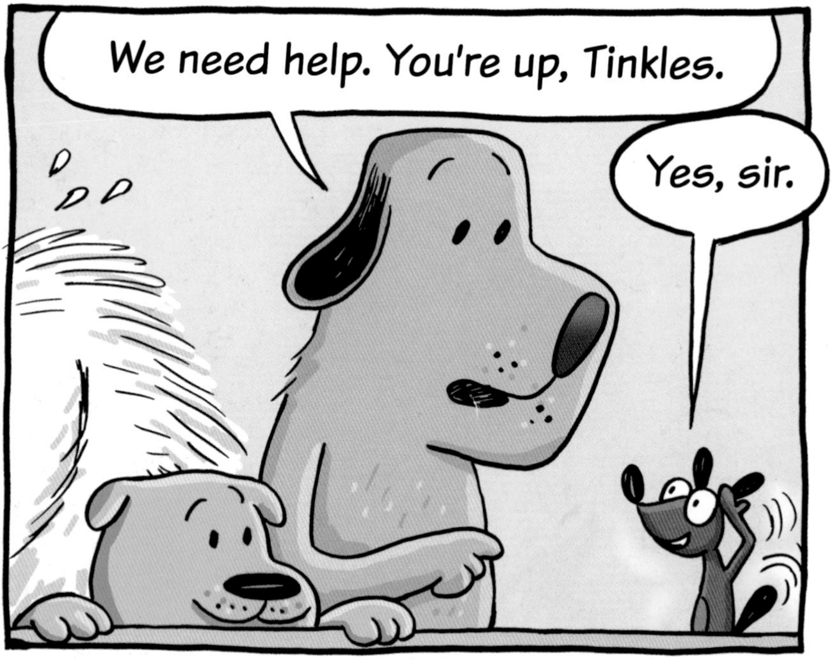
We need help. You're up, Tinkles.
Yes, sir.

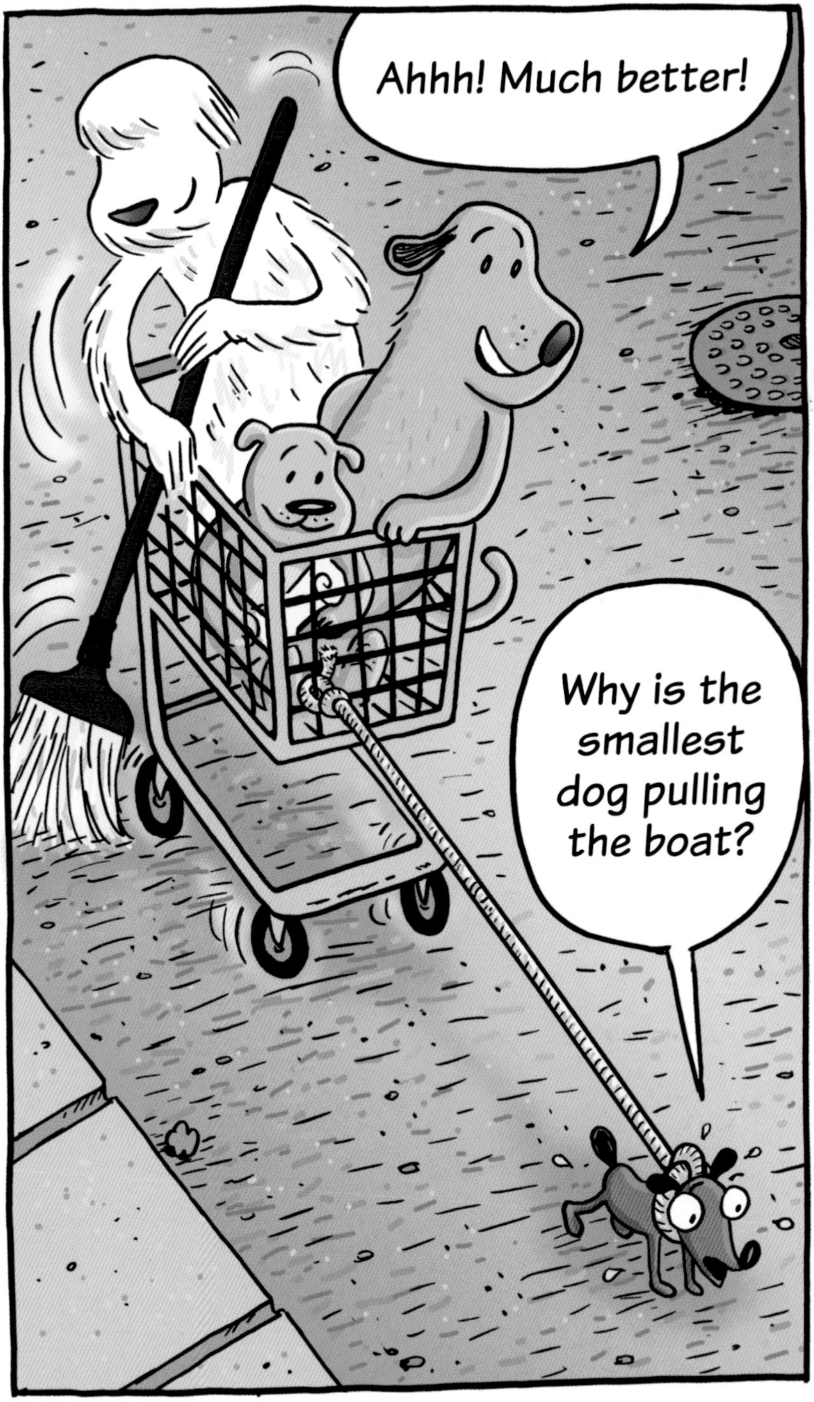
Ahhh! Much better!
Why is the smallest dog pulling the boat?

Following the map, Captain Hooktail led the pirates to the treasure.

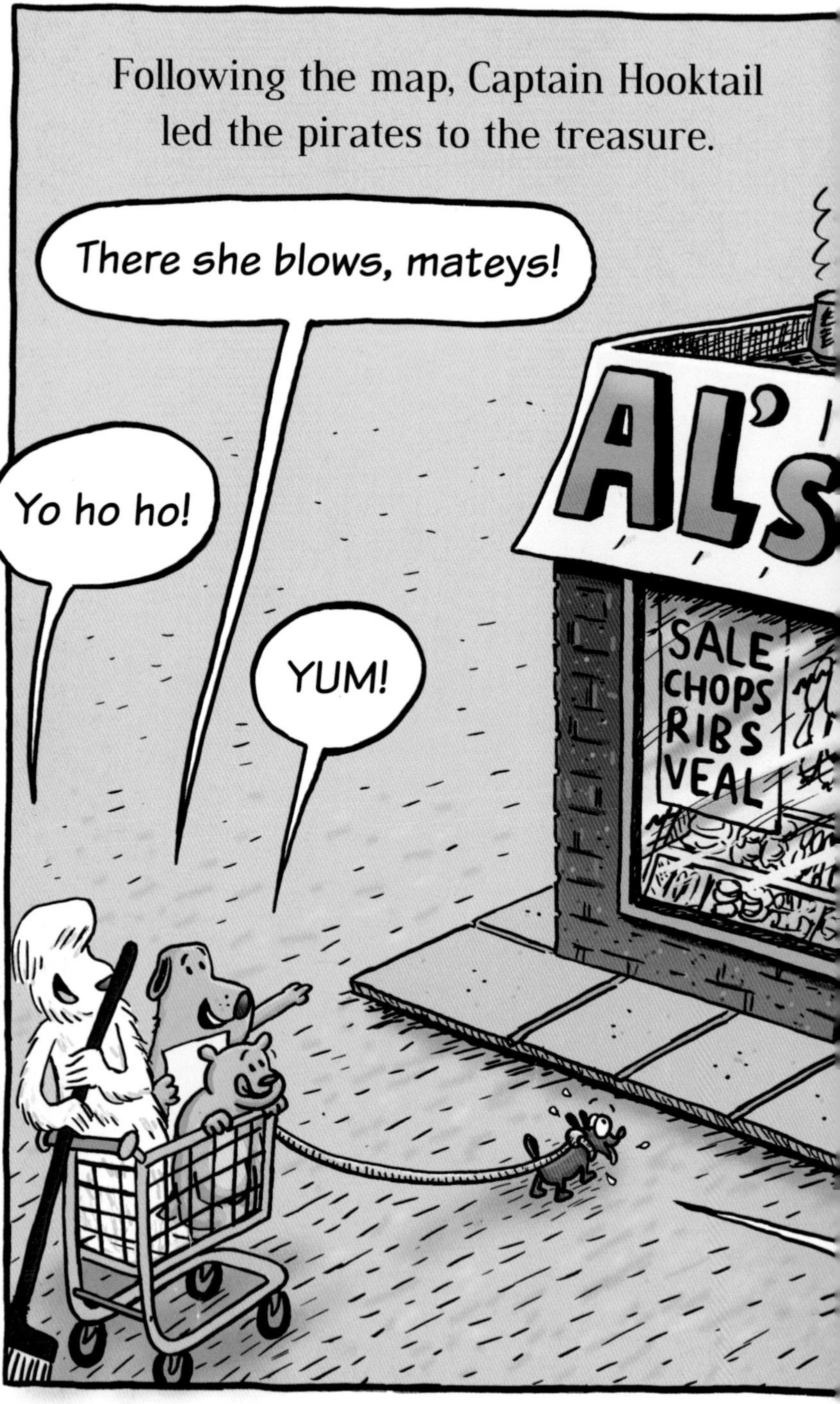
There she blows, mateys!
Yo ho ho!
YUM!
AL'S
SALE
CHOPS
RIBS
VEAL

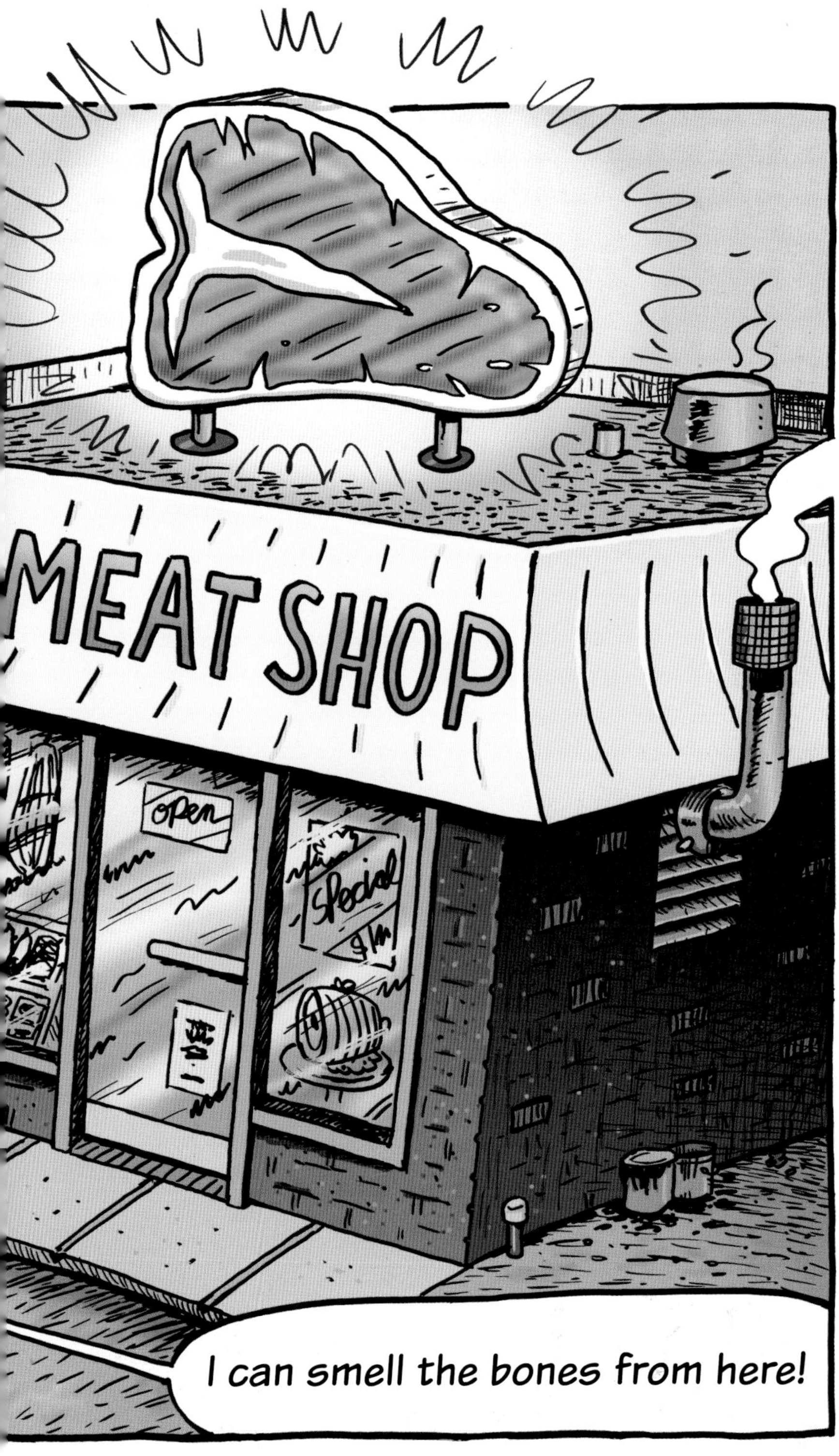
MEAT SHOP
open
Special
I can smell the bones from here!

Chapter Four

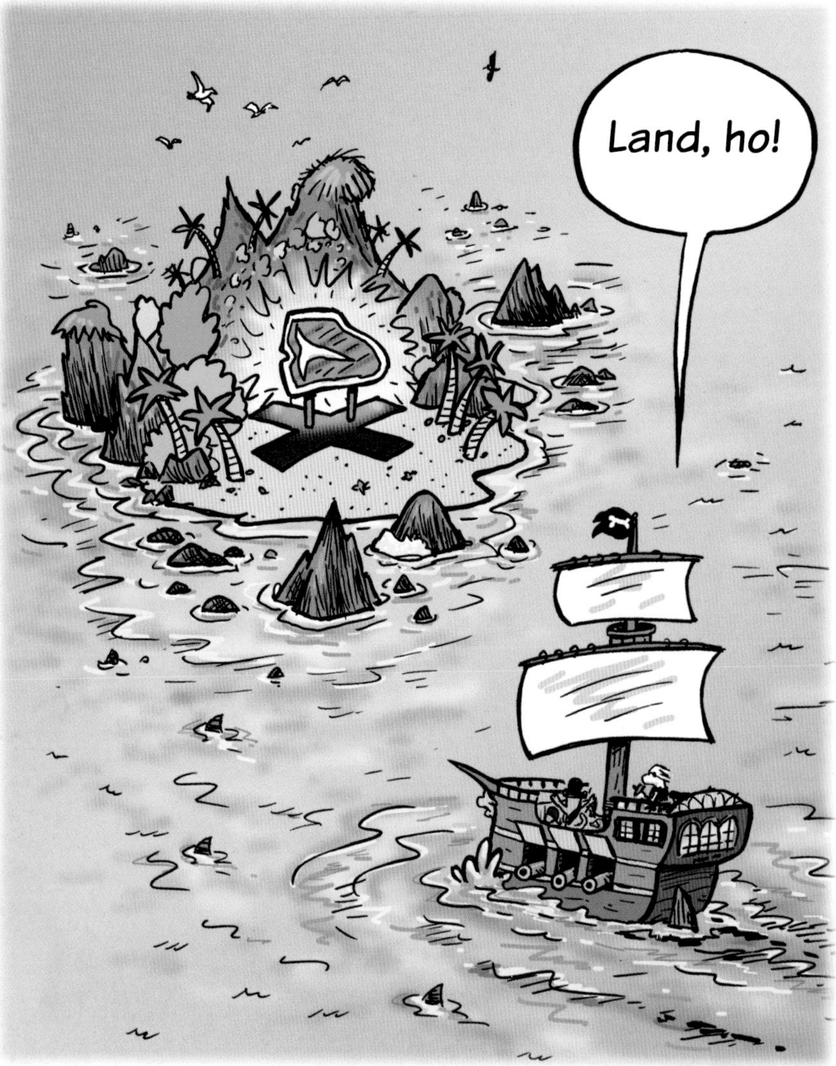
Land, ho!

The fearsome foursome spotted
Treasure Island.

They launched their attack.
Cannons blasted! Smoke billowed!
Cats fled in terror!

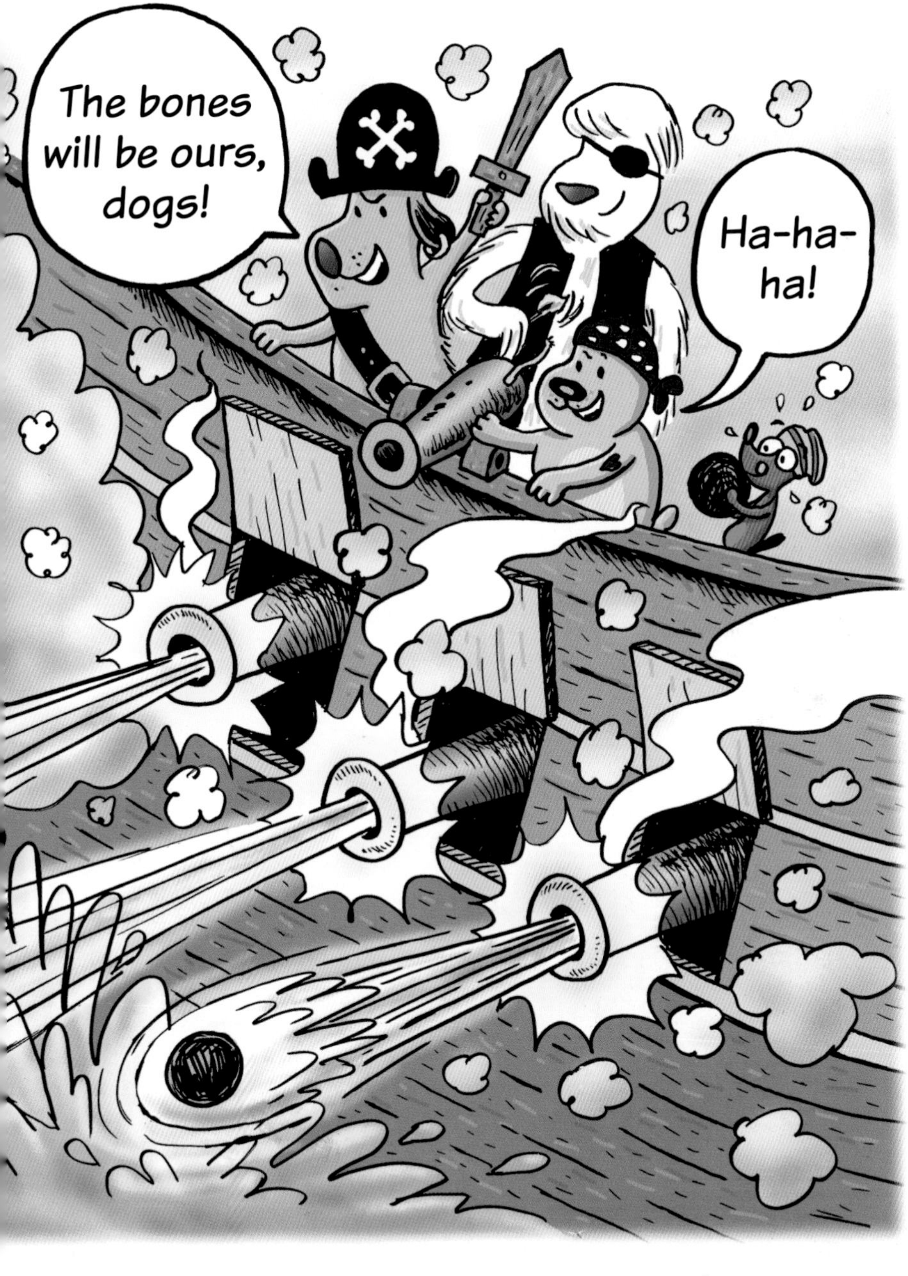
The bones will be ours, dogs!
Ha-ha-ha!

The dogs rushed at the meat shop.

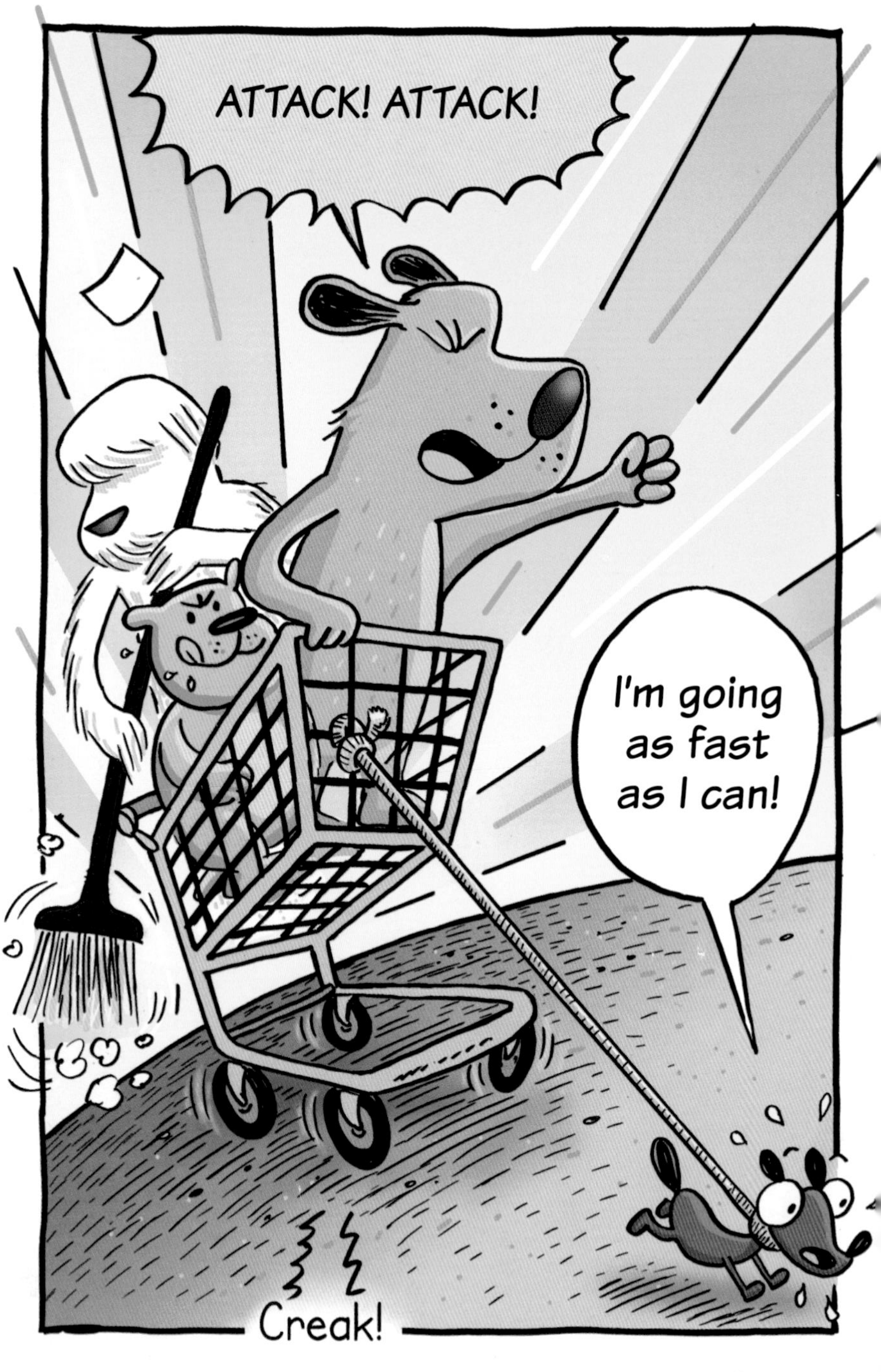

ATTACK! ATTACK!
I'm going as fast as I can!
Creak!

But suddenly they screeched to a stop.

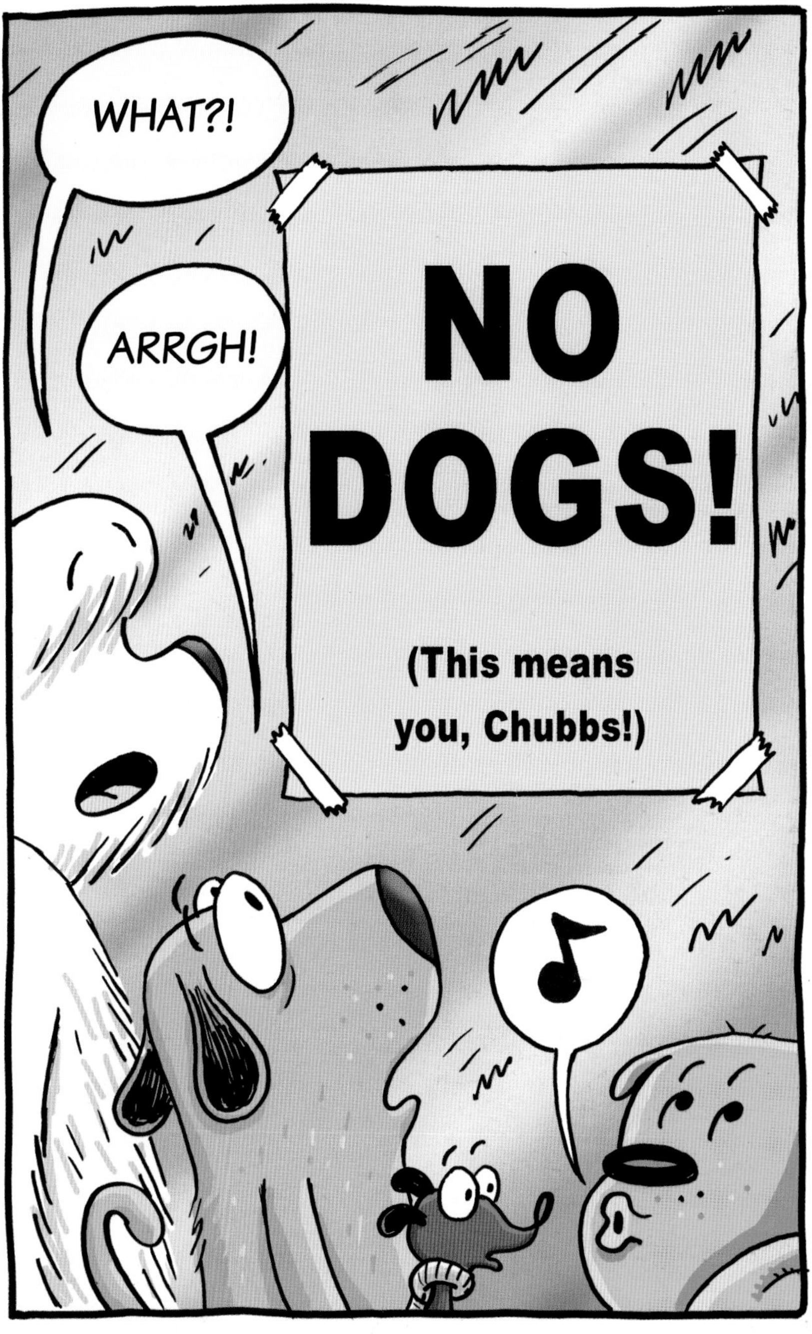
WHAT?!
ARRGH!
NO DOGS!
(This means you, Chubbs!)

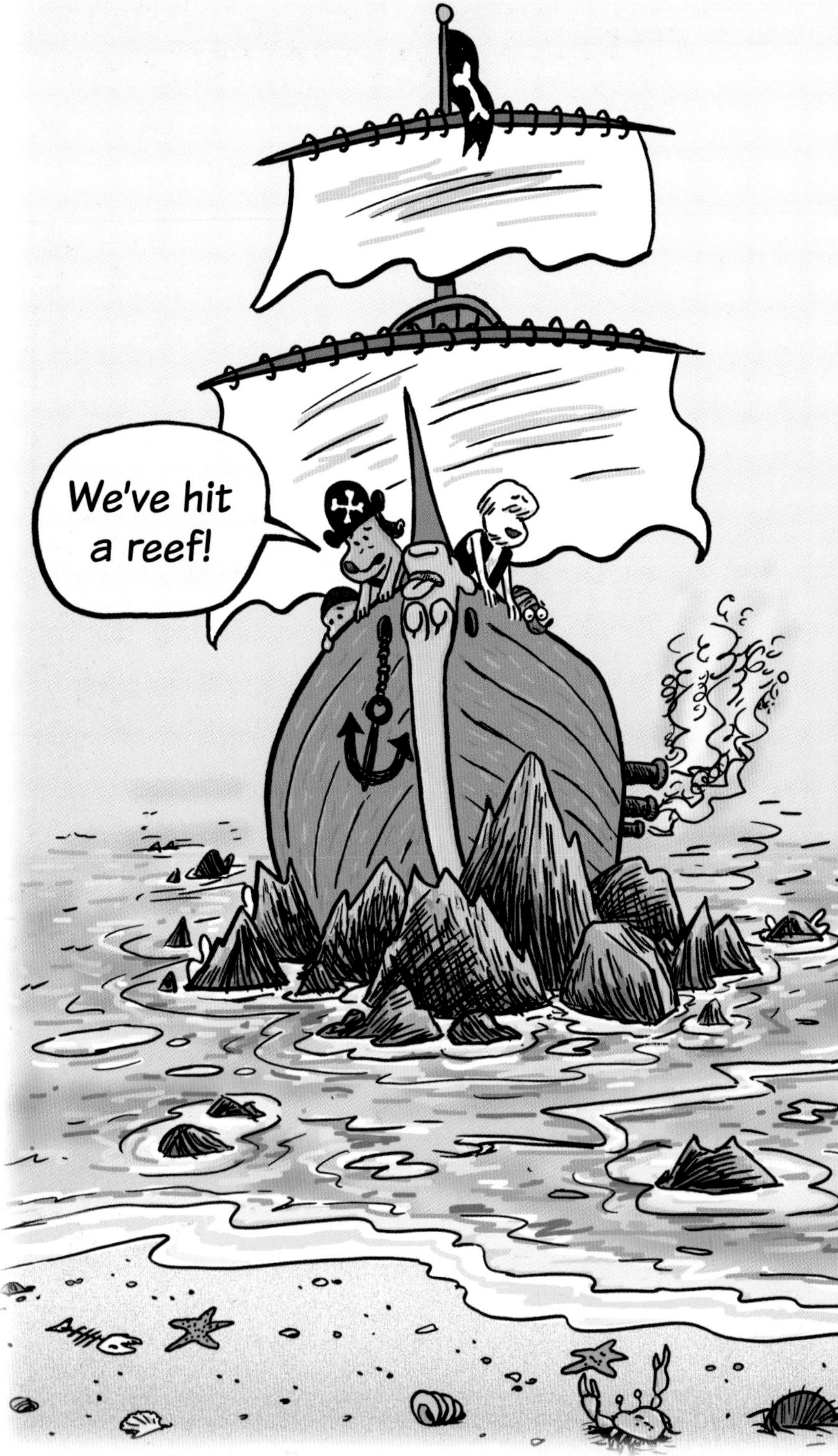
We've hit a reef!

Chapter Five

The Scurvy Dogs were stuck.

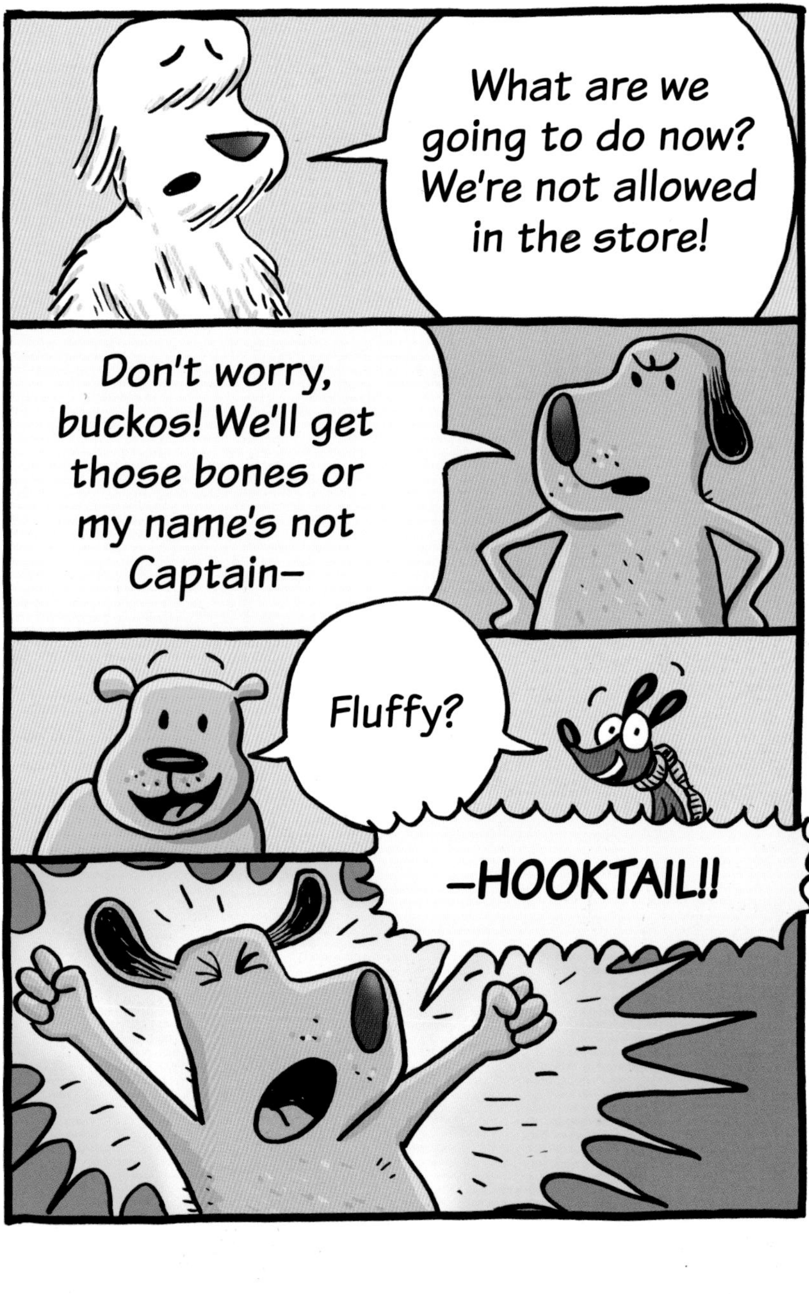
What are we going to do now? We're not allowed in the store!
Don't worry, buckos! We'll get those bones or my name's not Captain–
Fluffy?
–HOOKTAIL!!

Suddenly, Patch had an idea.

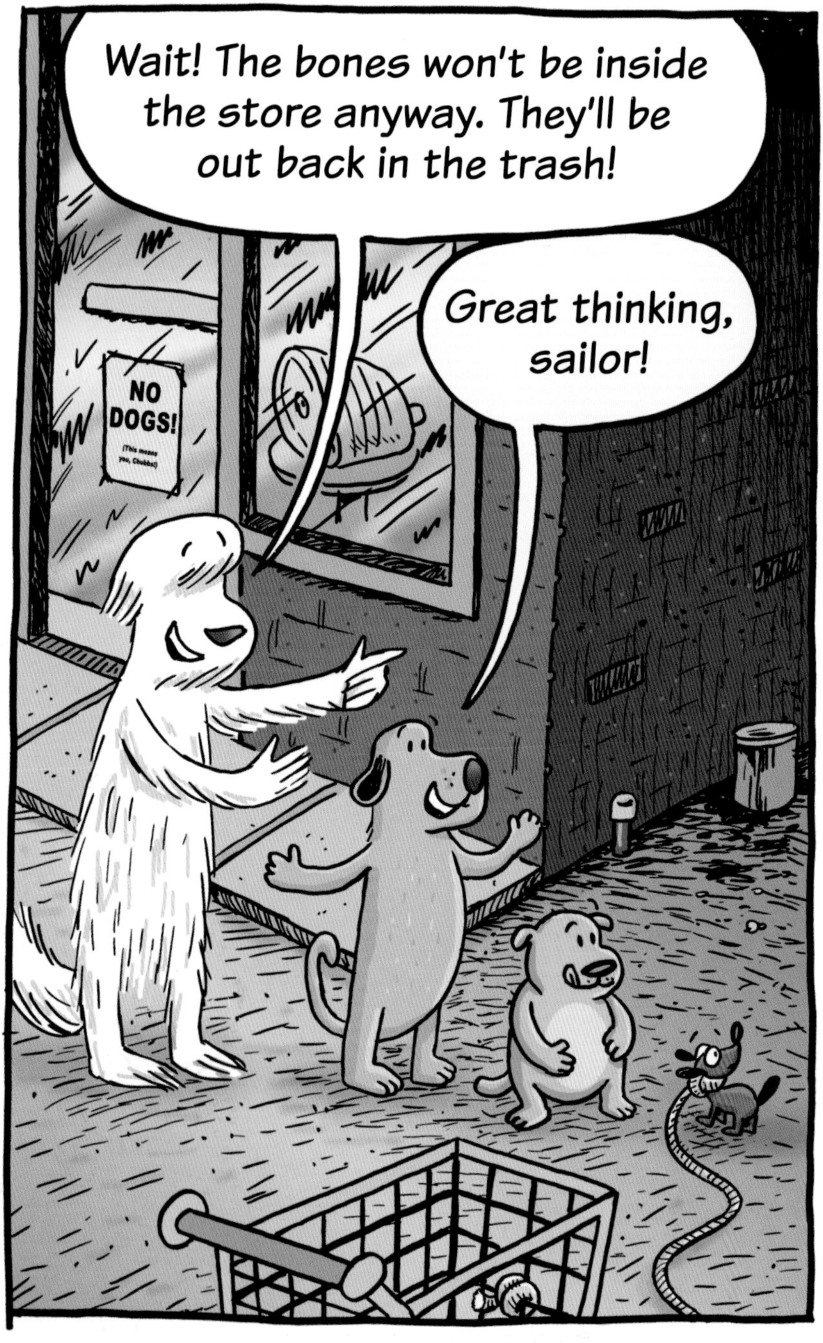
Wait! The bones won't be inside the store anyway. They'll be out back in the trash!
Great thinking, sailor!
NO DOGS!
(This means you, Chubbs!)

Patch steered the ship off the reef and sailed behind Treasure Island.

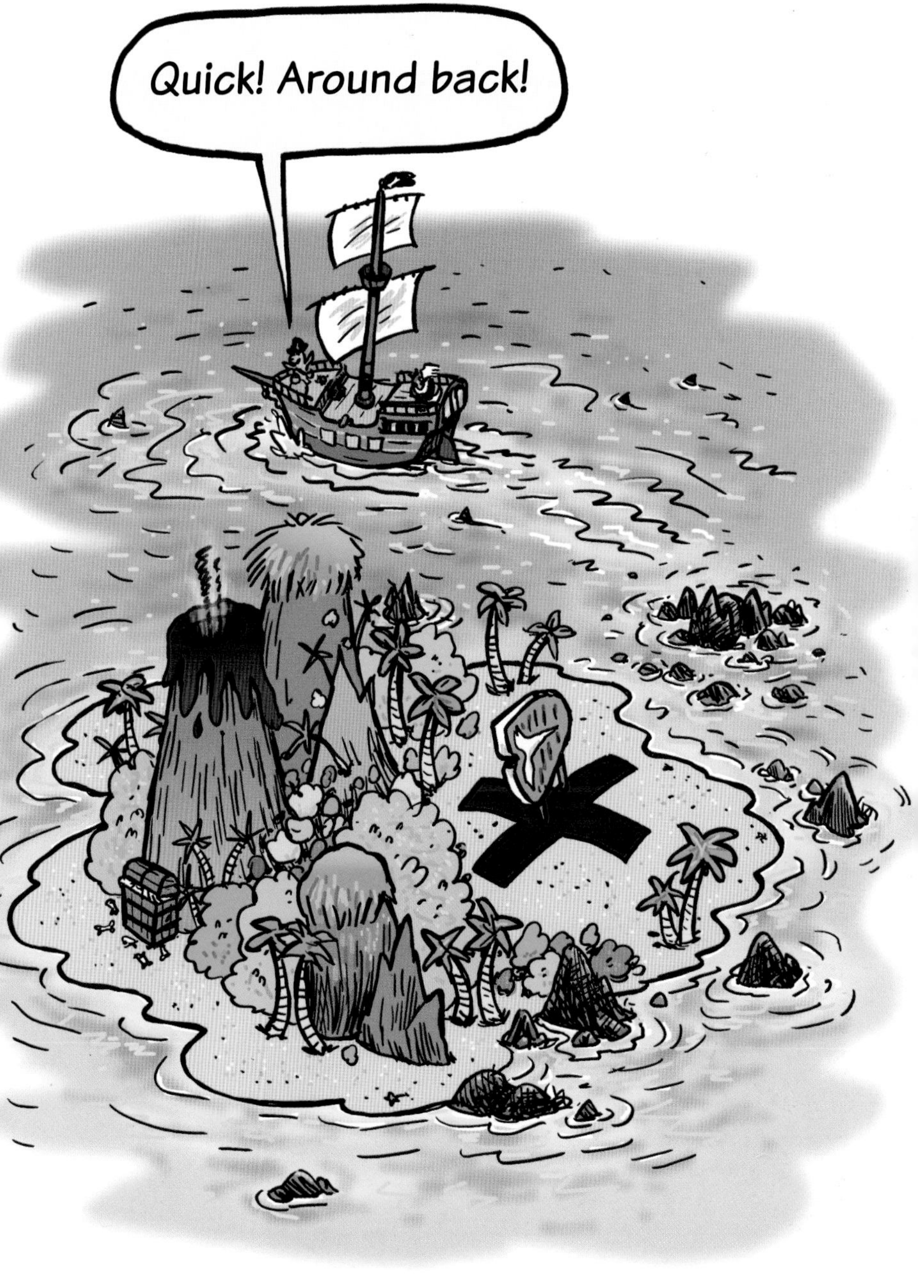
Quick! Around back!

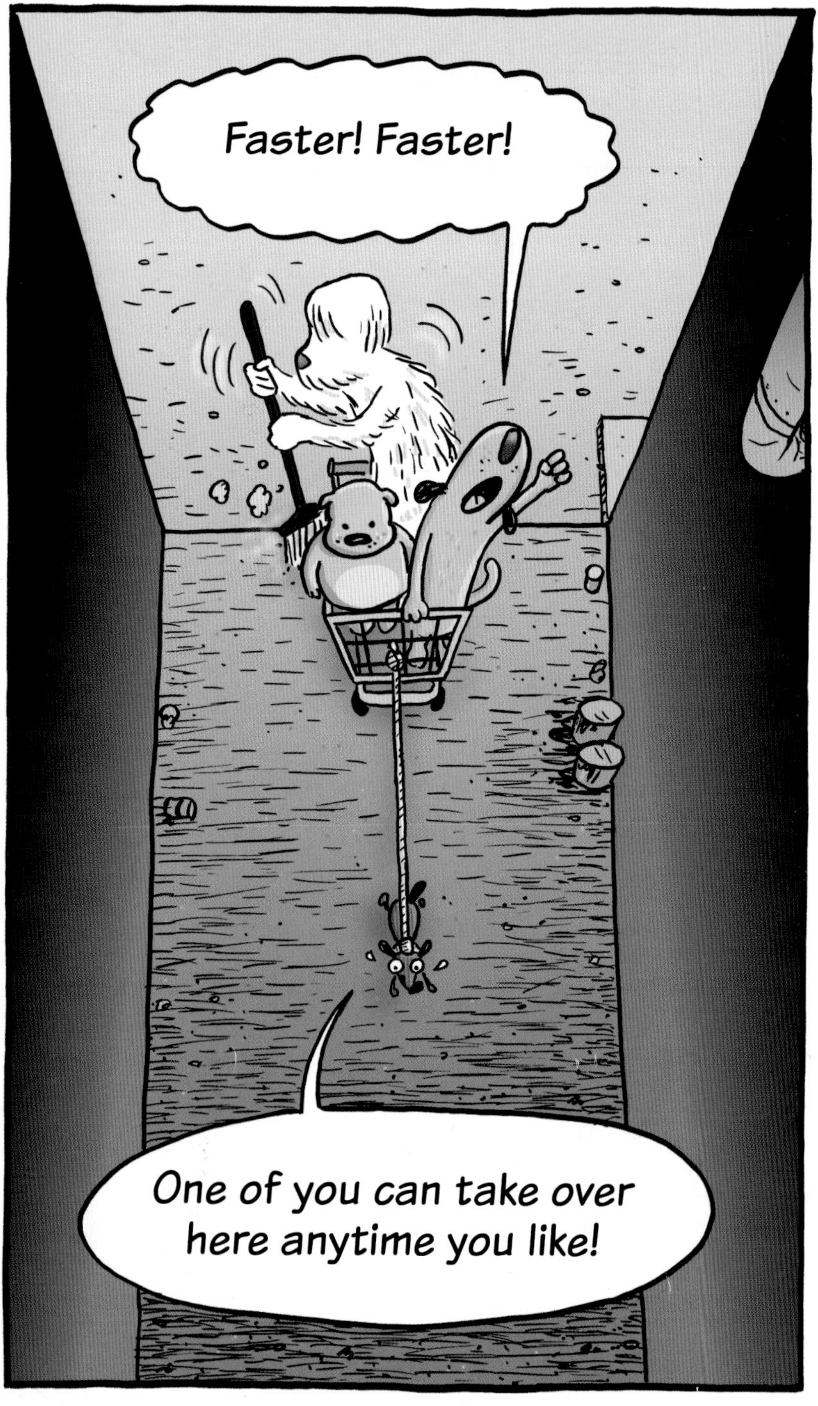
Faster! Faster!
One of you can take over here anytime you like!

There it is, mateys! The treasure!

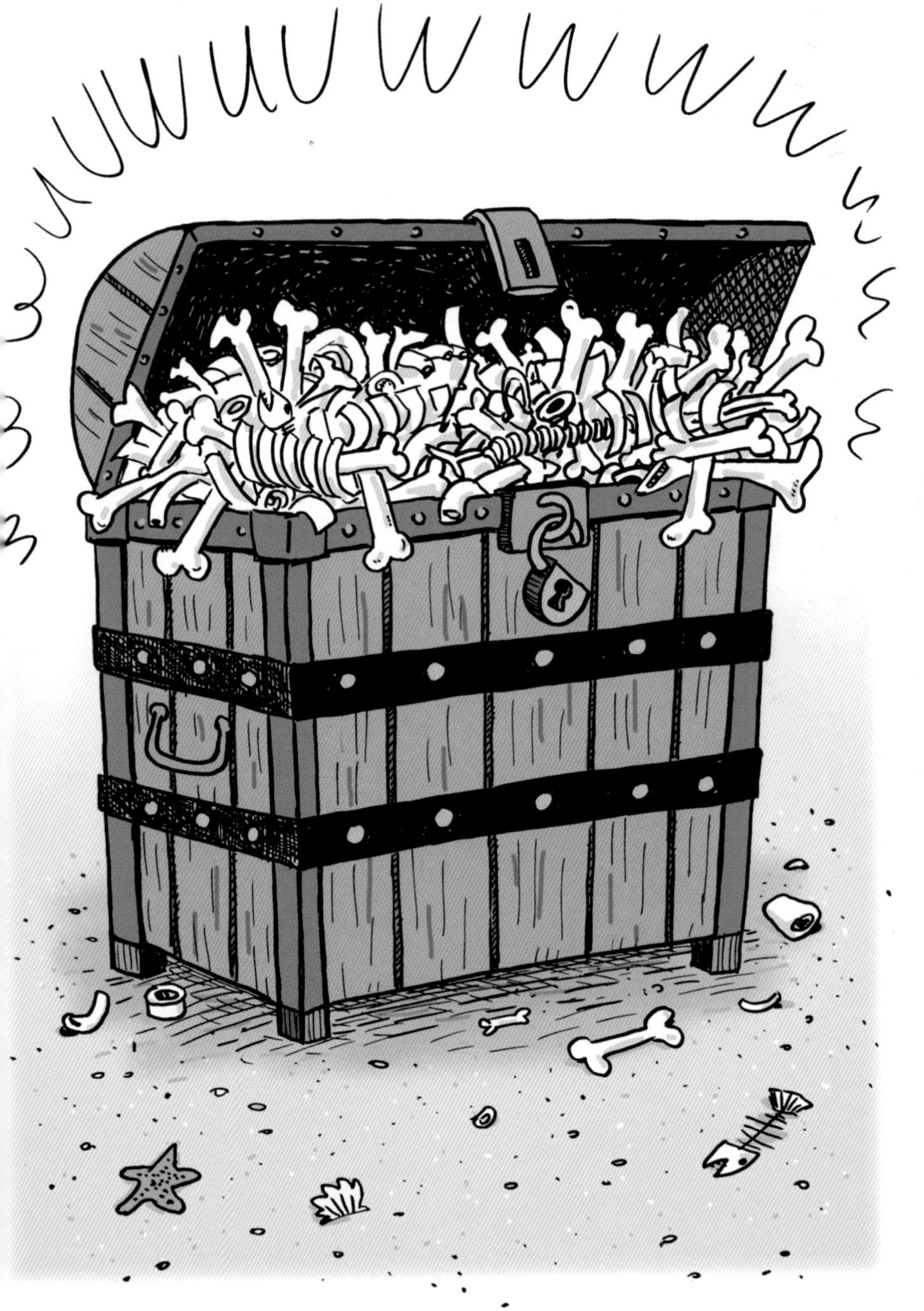

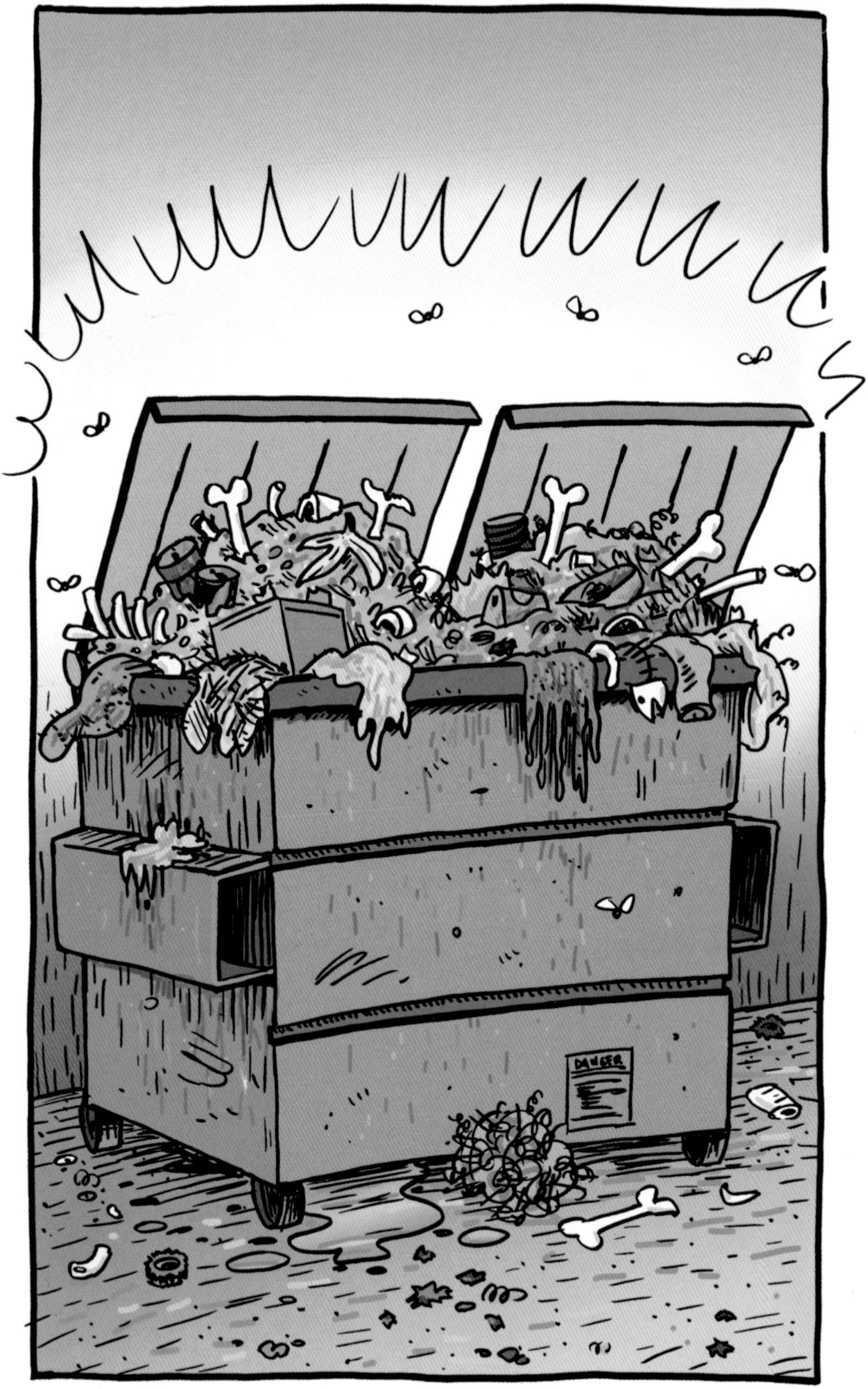
DANGER

They were overcome with emotion.

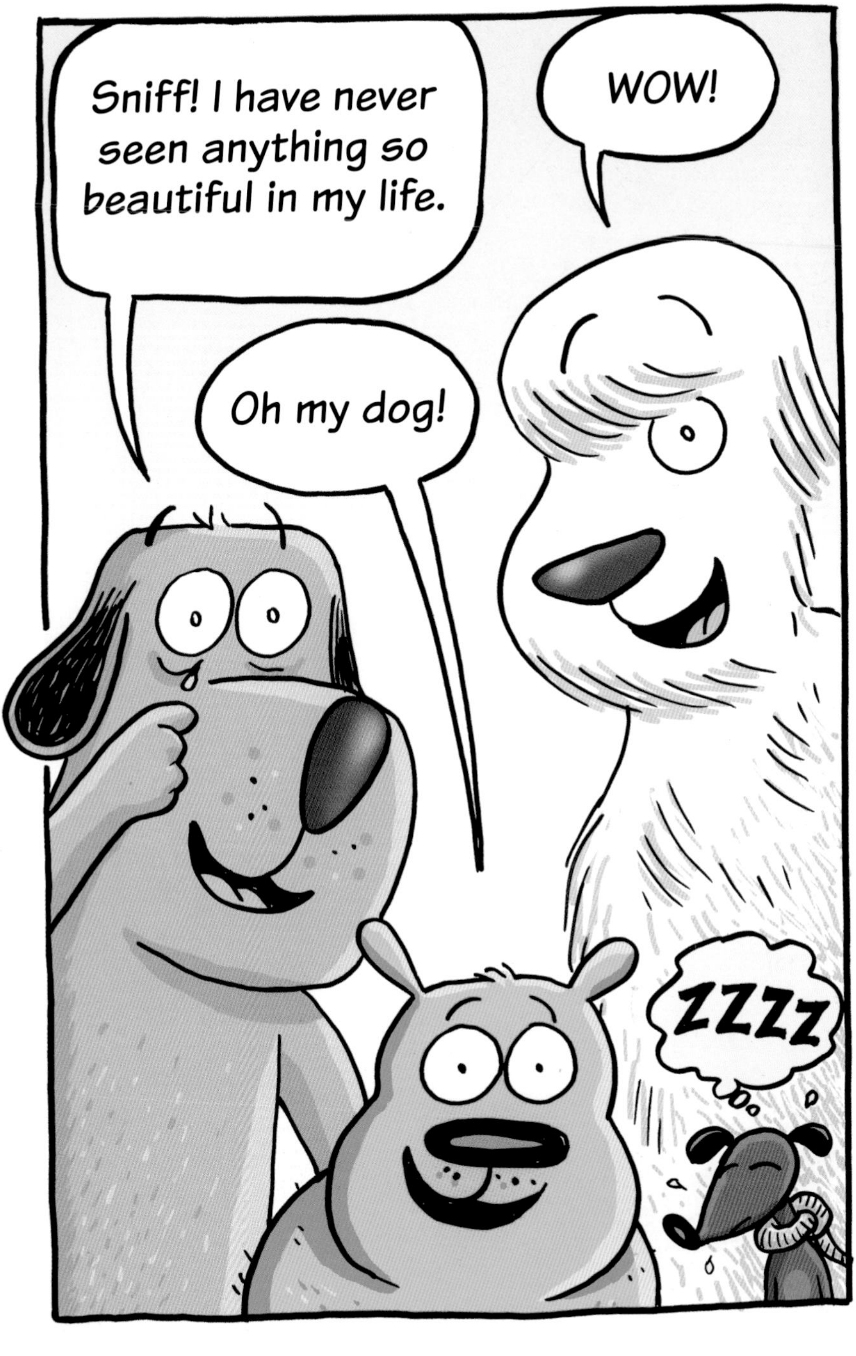
Sniff! I have never seen anything so beautiful in my life.
WOW!
Oh my dog!
ZZZZ

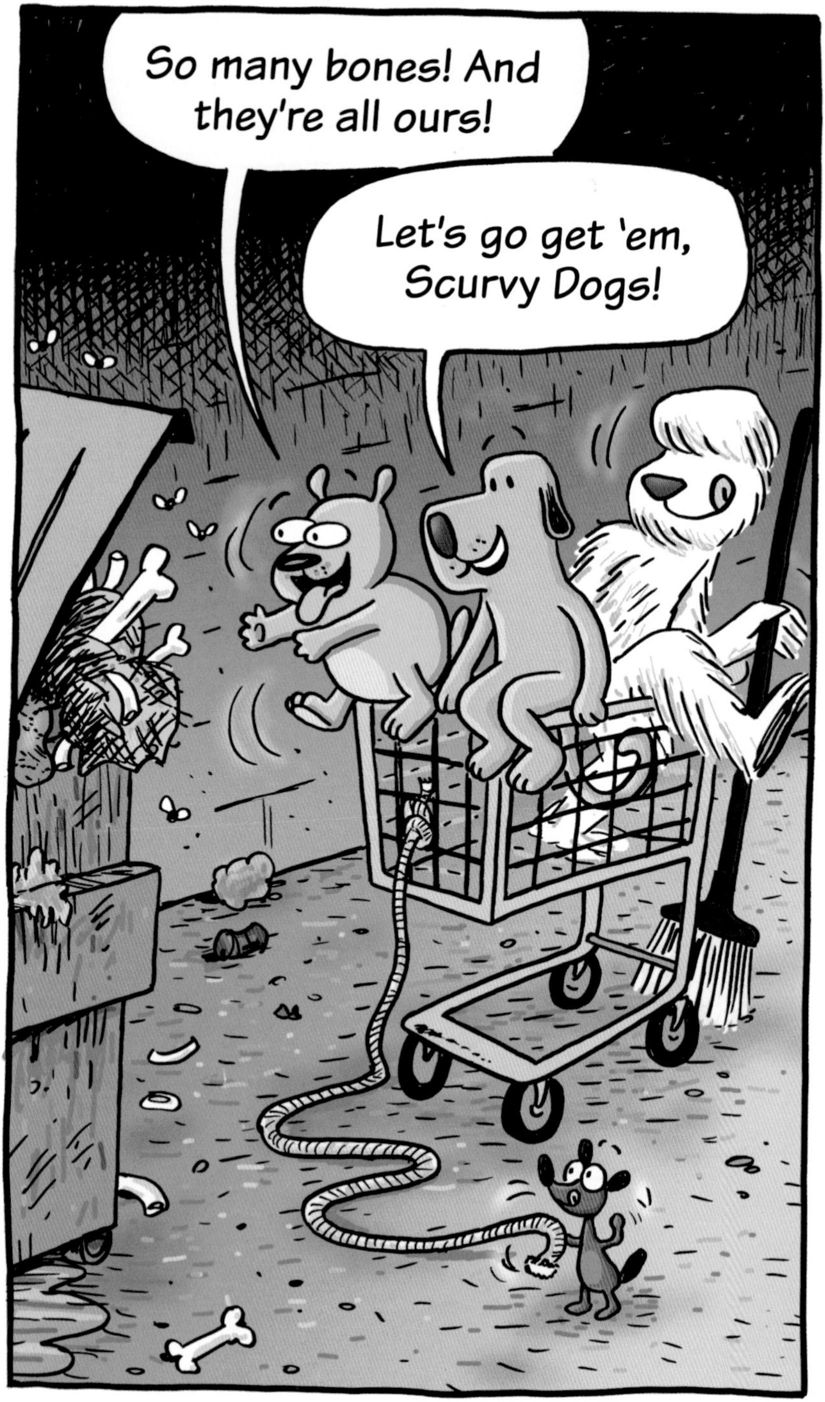
So many bones! And they're all ours!
Let's go get 'em, Scurvy Dogs!

When suddenly …

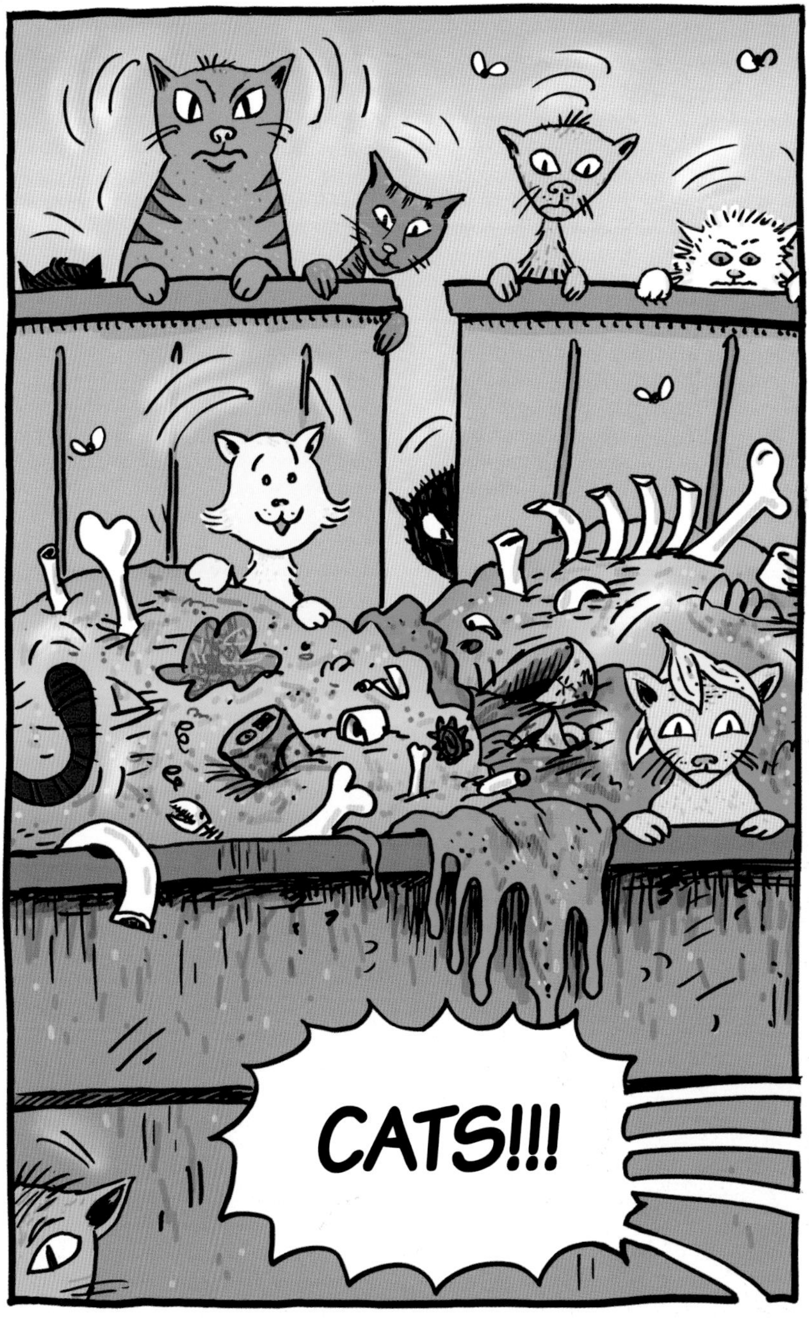
CATS!!!

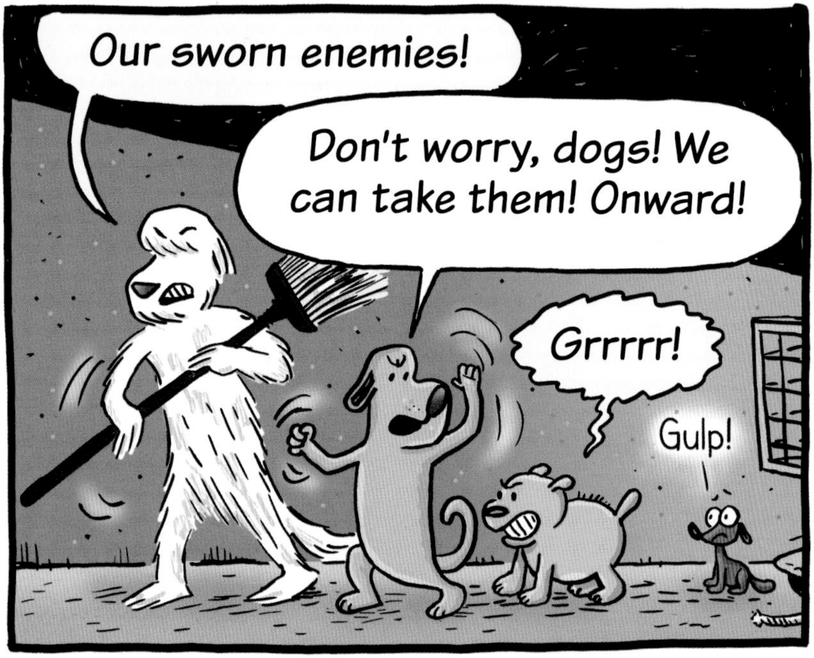
Our sworn enemies!
Don't worry, dogs! We can take them! Onward!
Grrrrr!
Gulp!

But then a cat stood up.

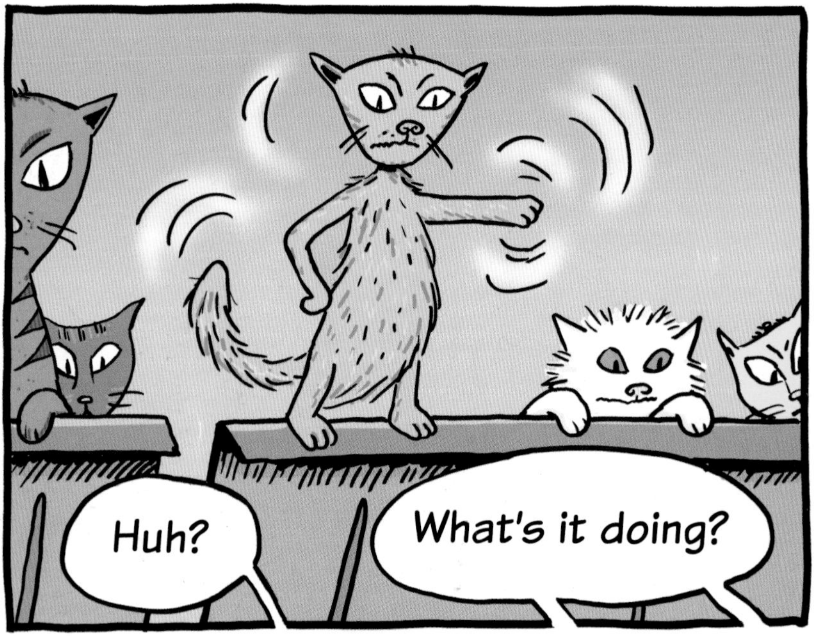
Huh?
What's it doing?

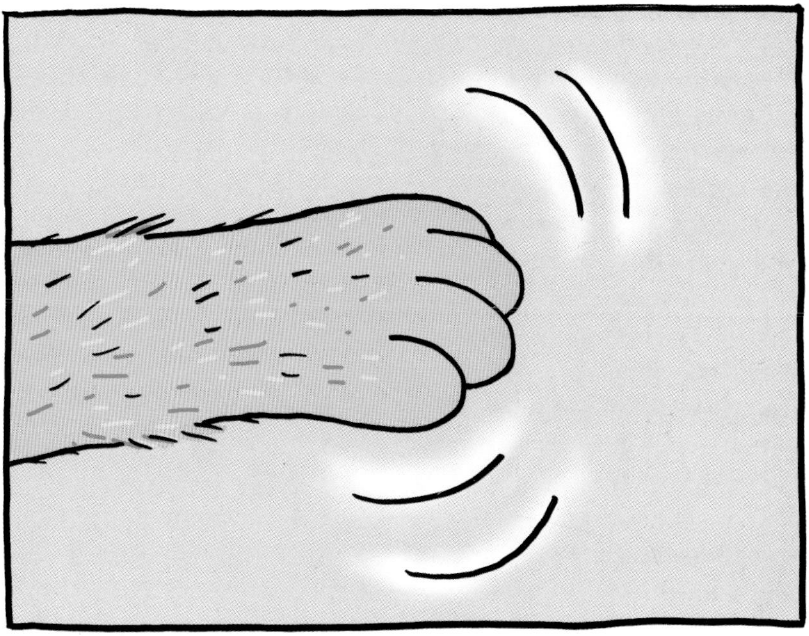

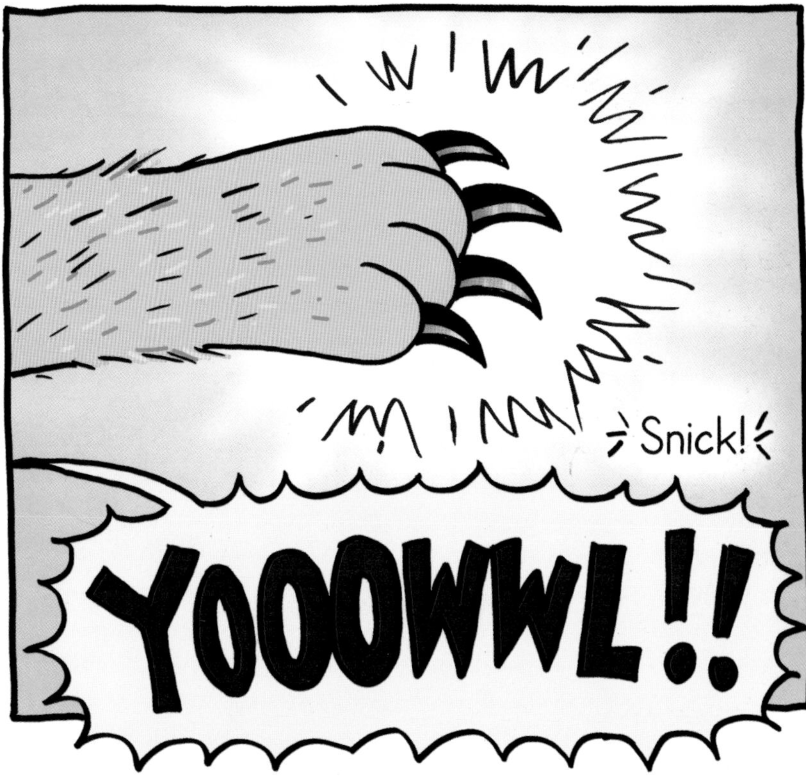
Snick!
YOOOWWL!!

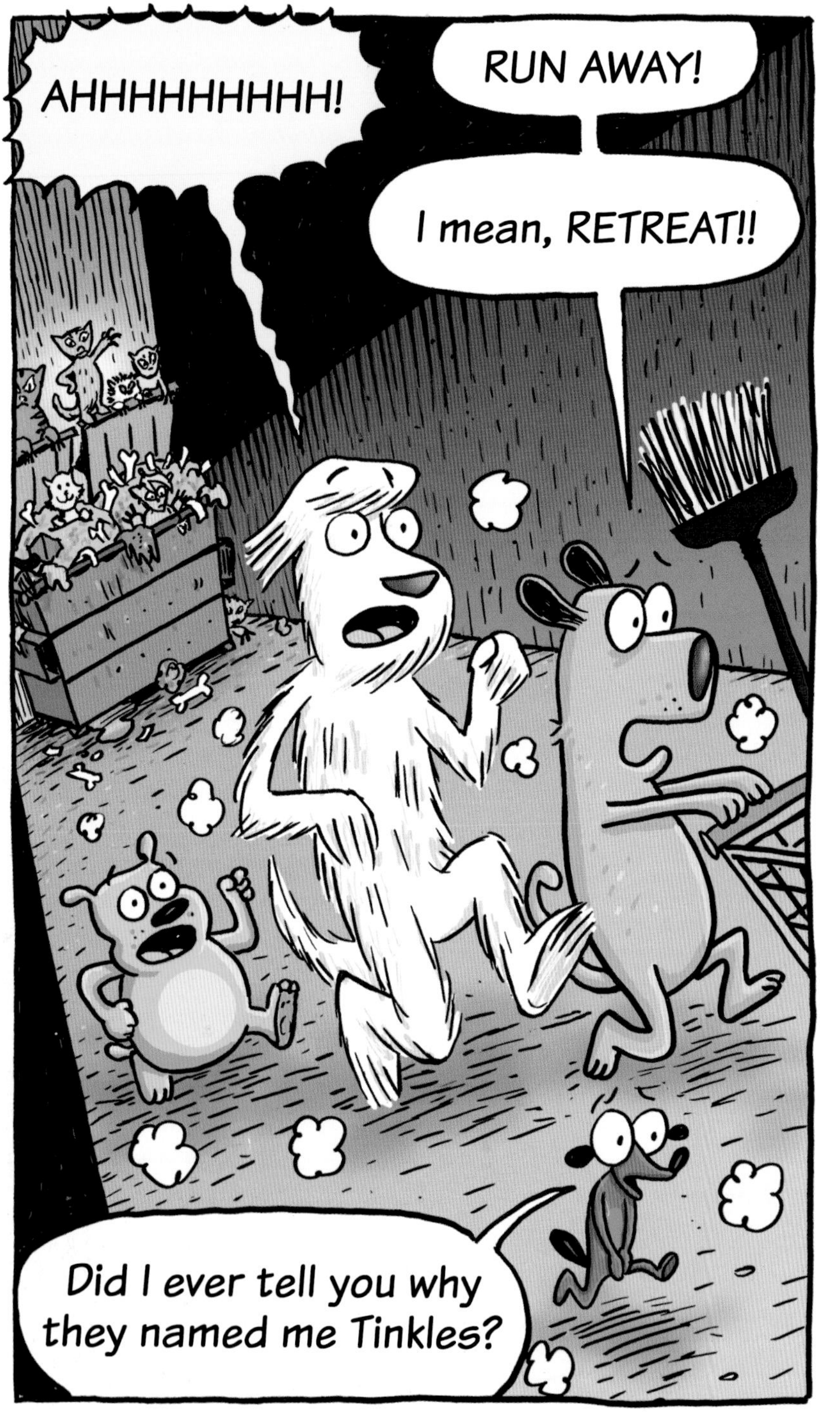
AHHHHHHHHHH!
RUN AWAY!
I mean, RETREAT!!
Did I ever tell you why
they named me Tinkles?

Treasure Island was protected by awful monsters, so the pirates had no choice but to abandon their quest and sail away.

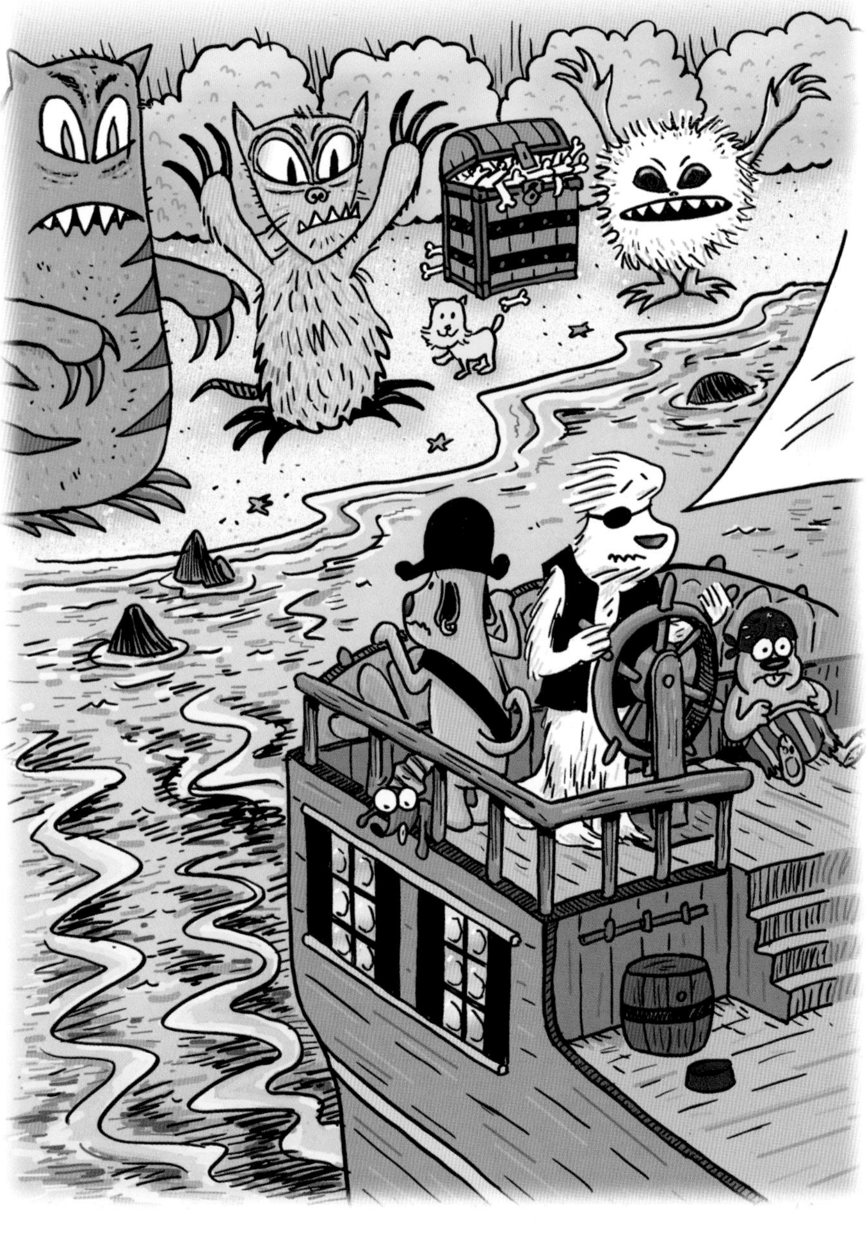

Chapter Six

The dogs wandered through town, feeling sad.

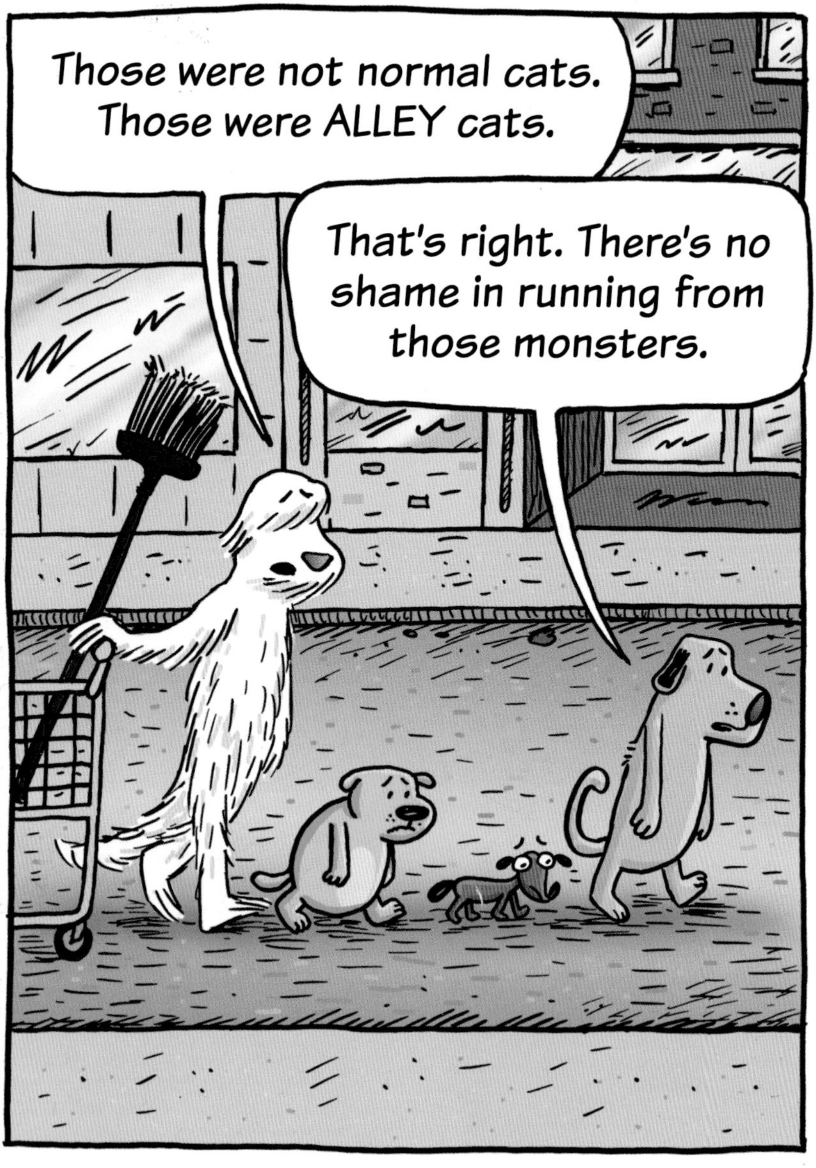
Those were not normal cats. Those were ALLEY cats.
That's right. There's no shame in running from those monsters.

But just when they were about to give up hope of ever finding some bones ...

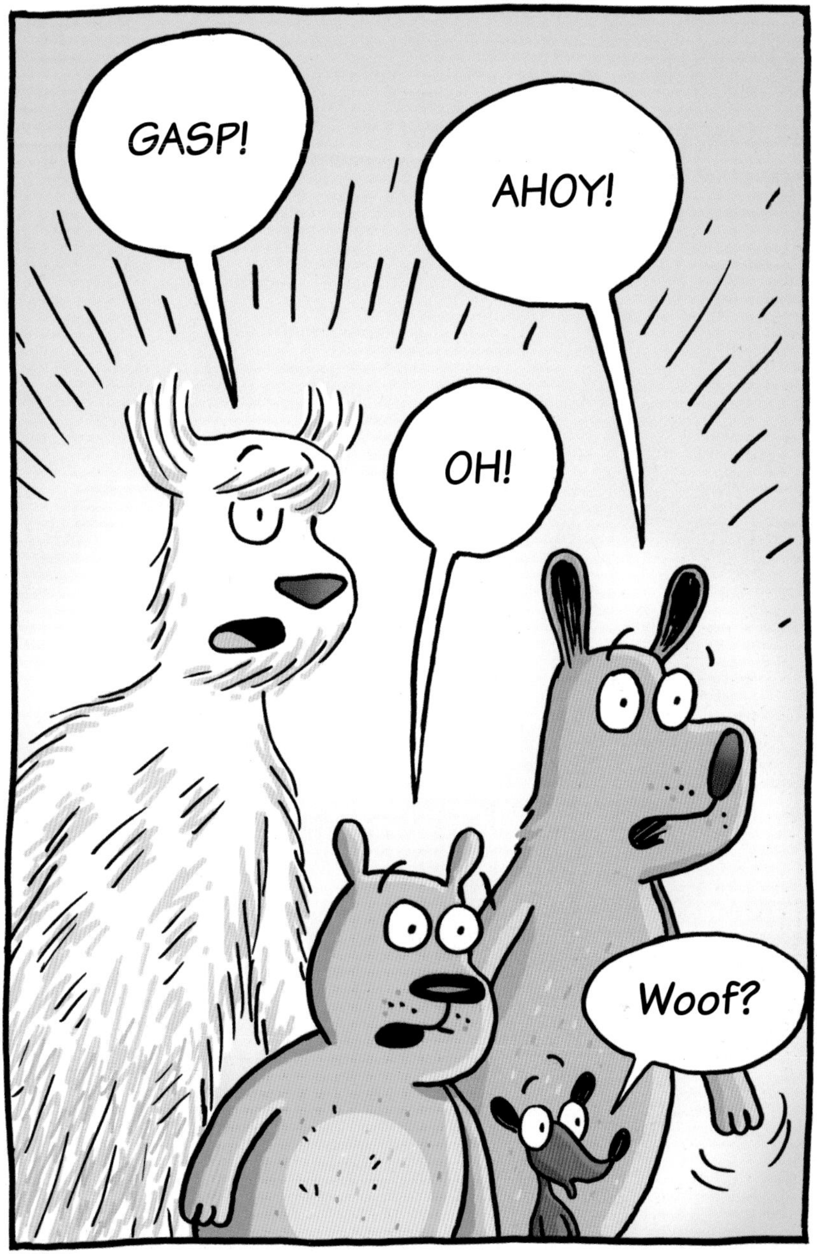
GASP!
AHOY!
OH!
Woof?

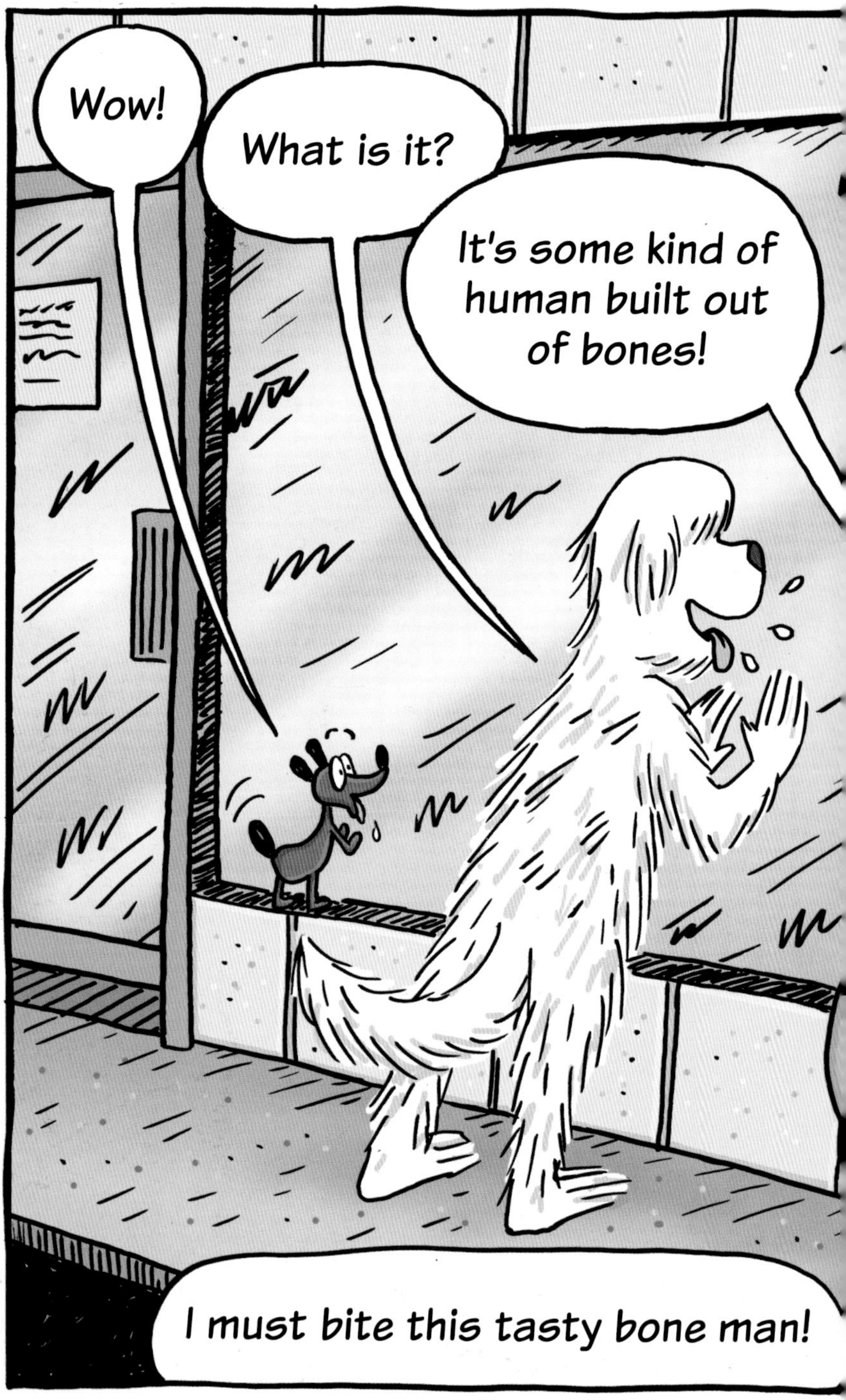
Wow!
What is it?
It's some kind of human built out of bones!
I must bite this tasty bone man!

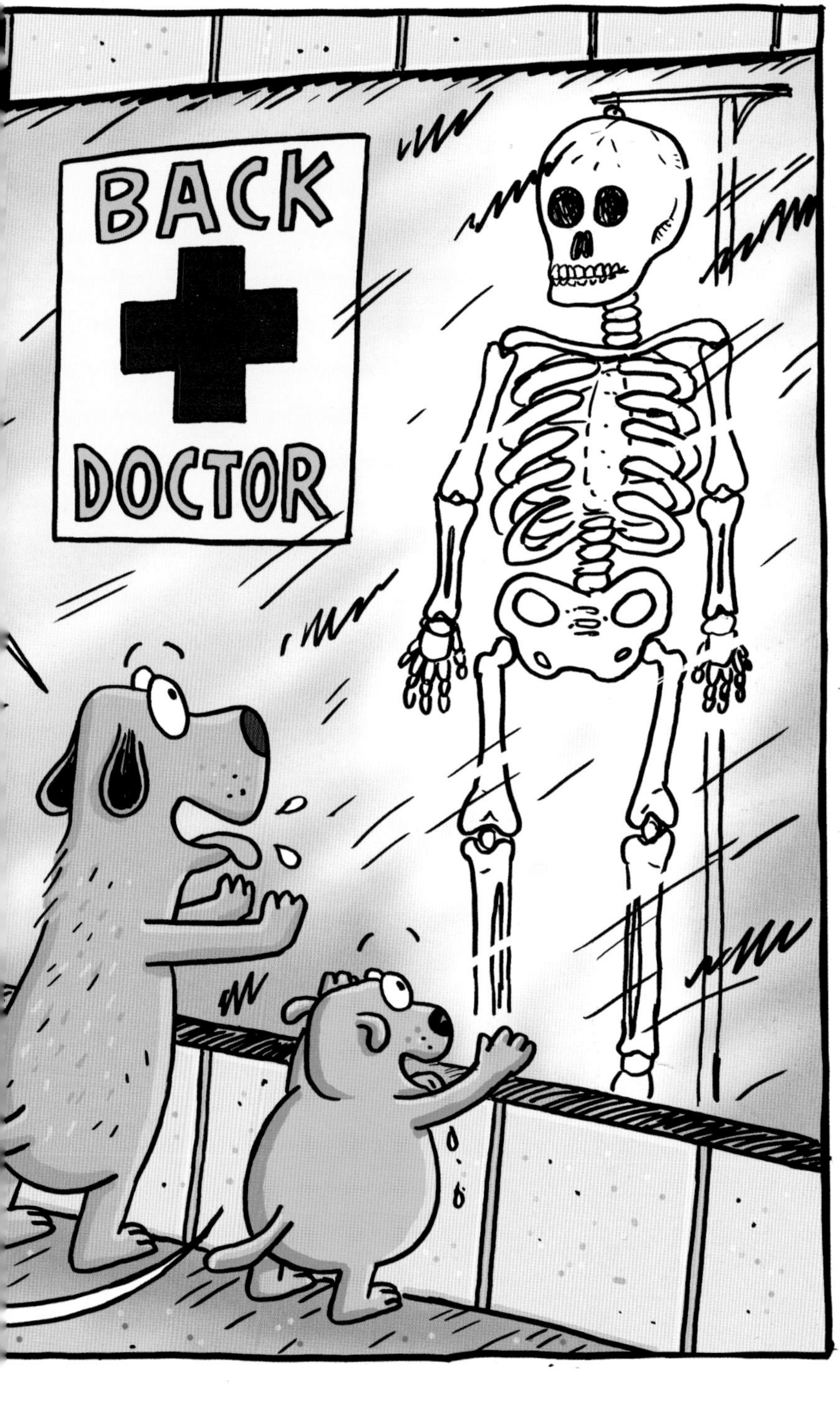
BACK
DOCTOR

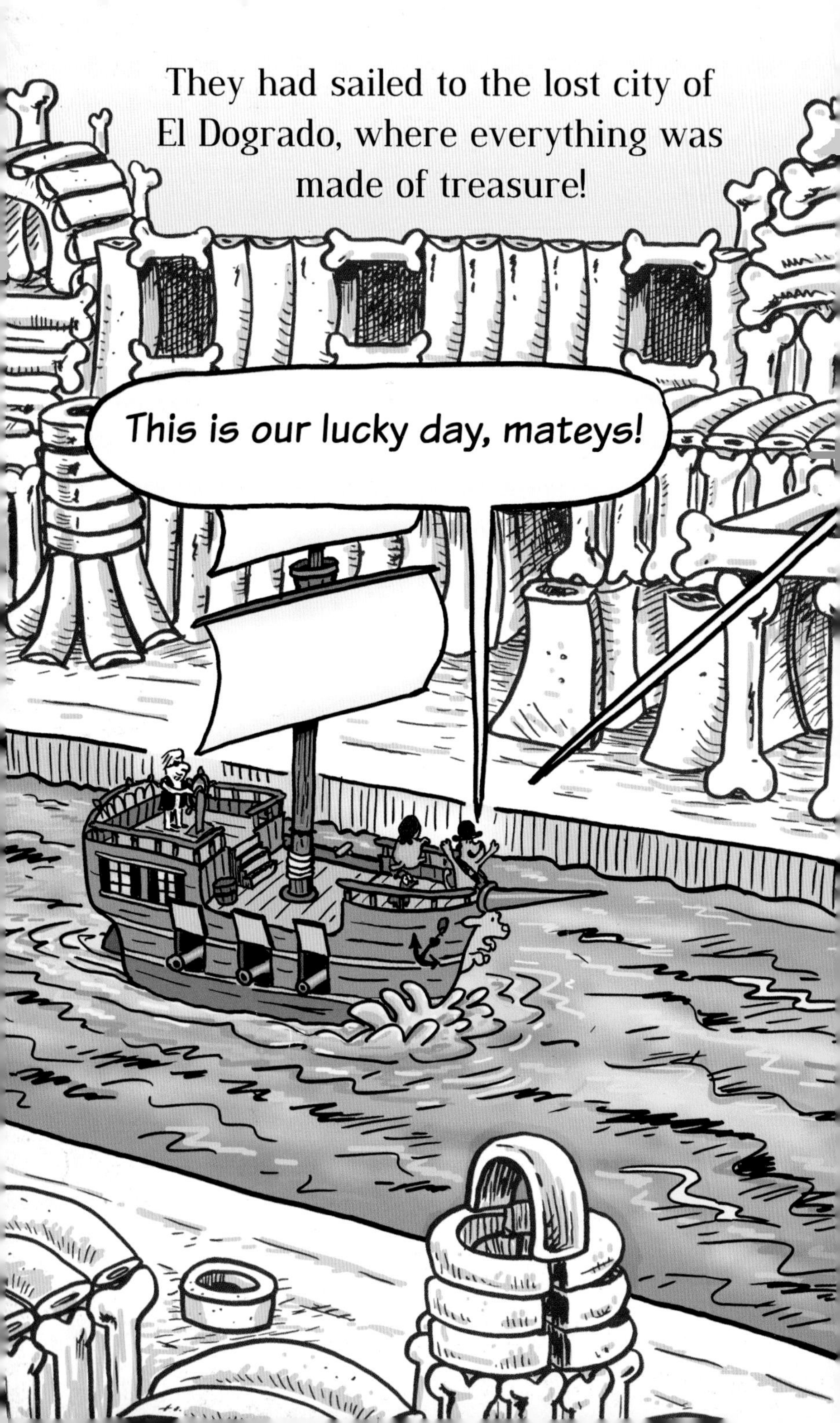
They had sailed to the lost city of El Dogrado, where everything was made of treasure!
This is our lucky day, mateys!

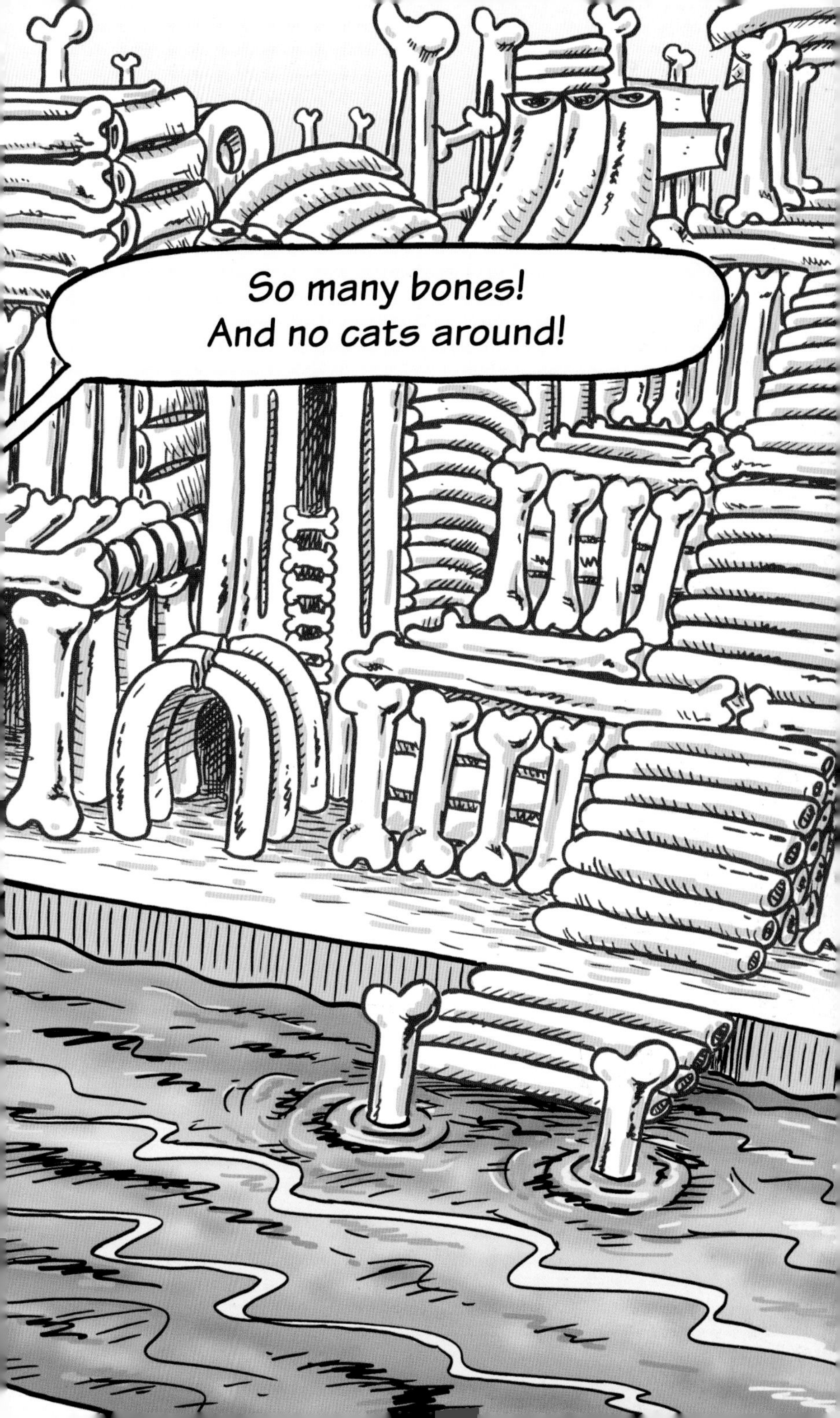
So many bones!
And no cats around!

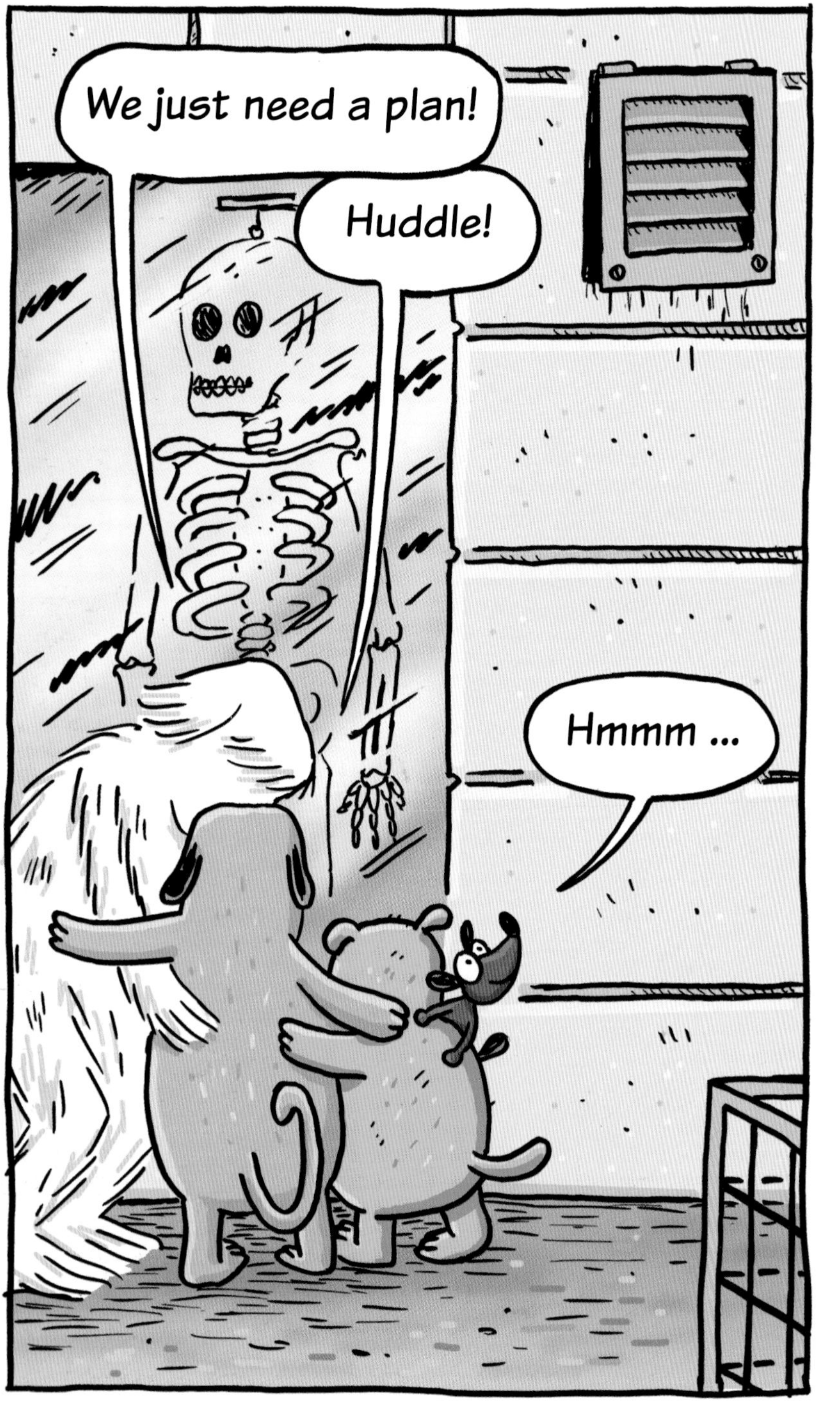
We just need a plan!
Huddle!
Hmmm ...

In no time at all, the clever dogs had come up with a very piratey plan.

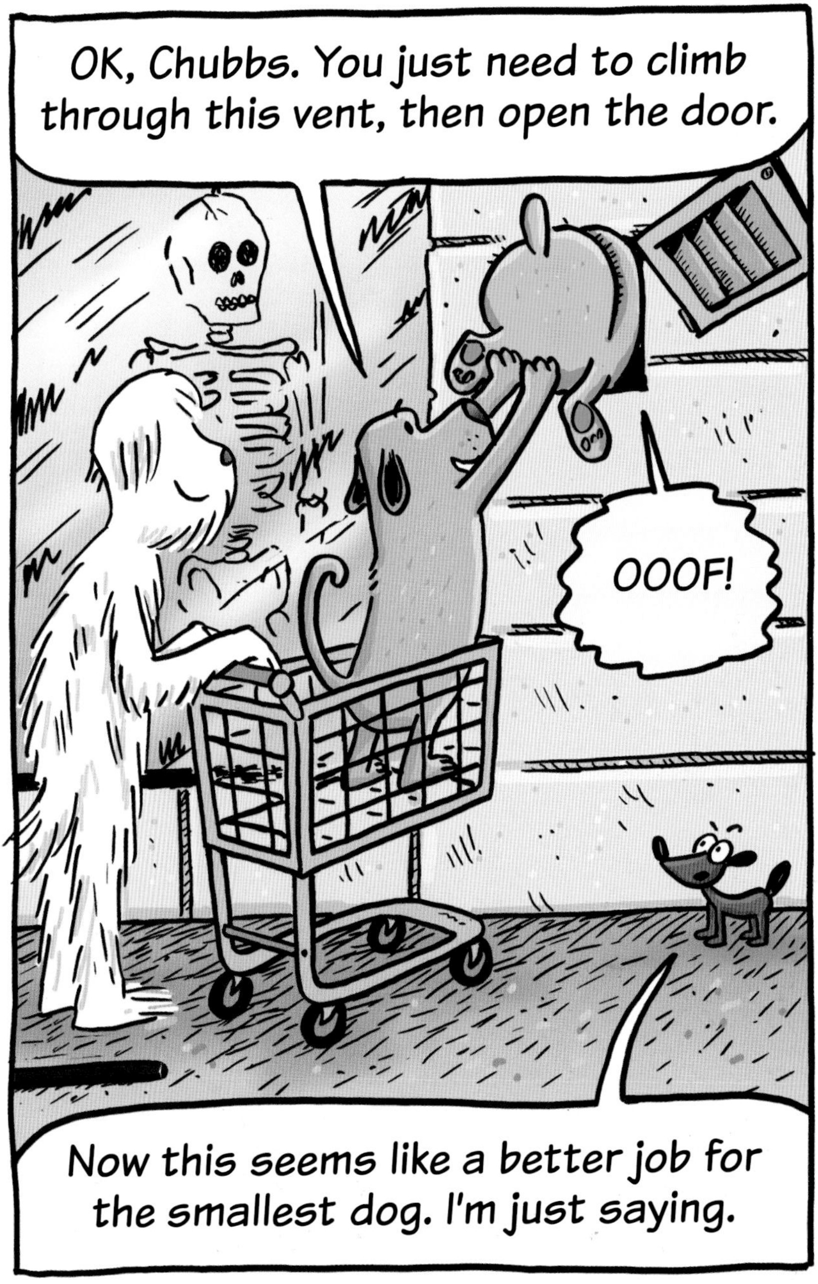
OK, Chubbs. You just need to climb through this vent, then open the door.
OOOF!
Now this seems like a better job for the smallest dog. I'm just saying.

Chubbs crawled through the narrow passage. But suddenly, the walls began to press in on him.

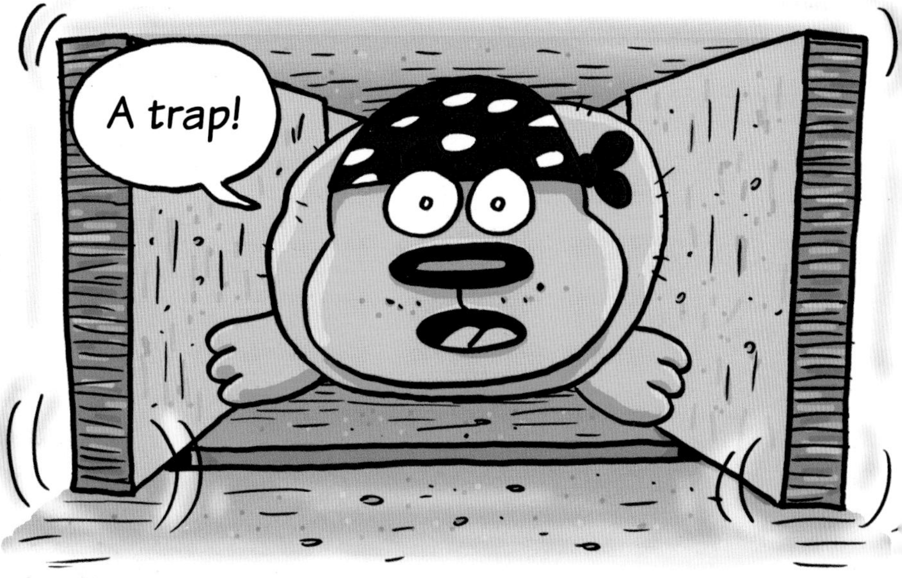
A trap!

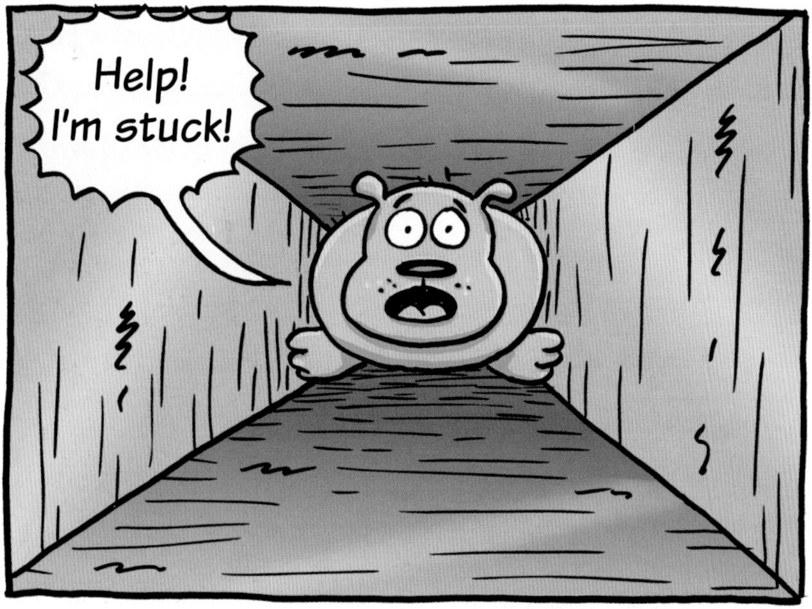
Help! I'm stuck!

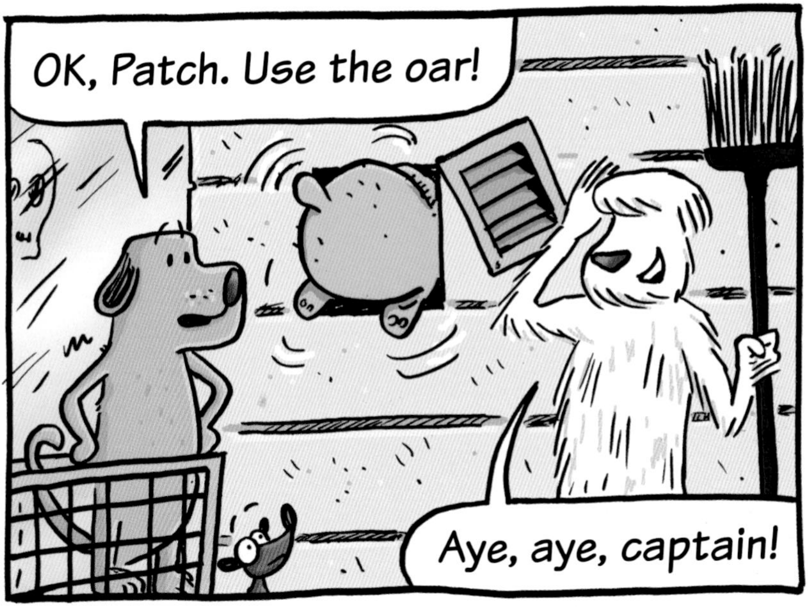
OK, Patch. Use the oar!
Aye, aye, captain!

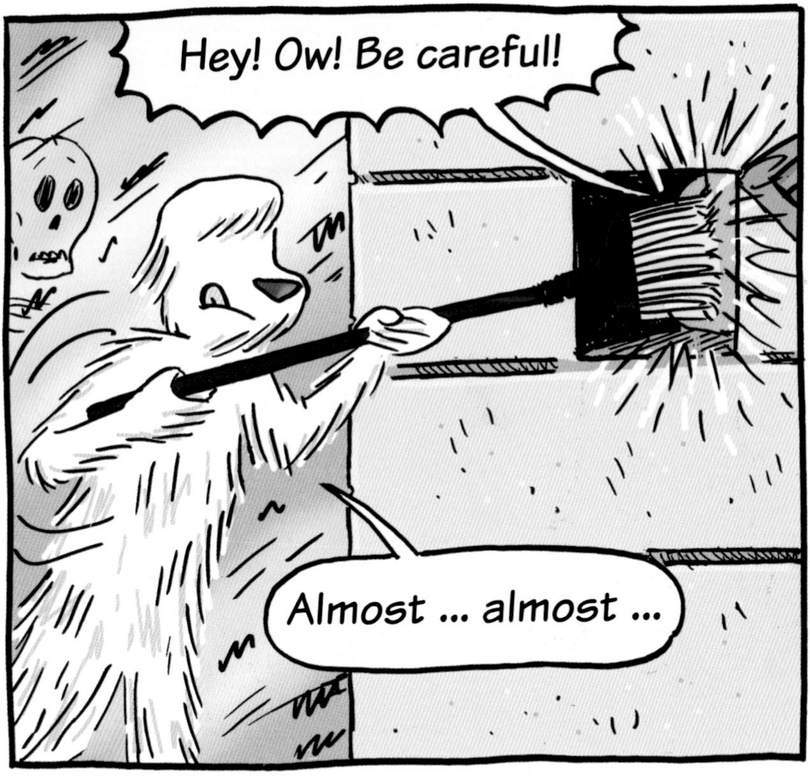
Hey! Ow! Be careful!
Almost ... almost ...

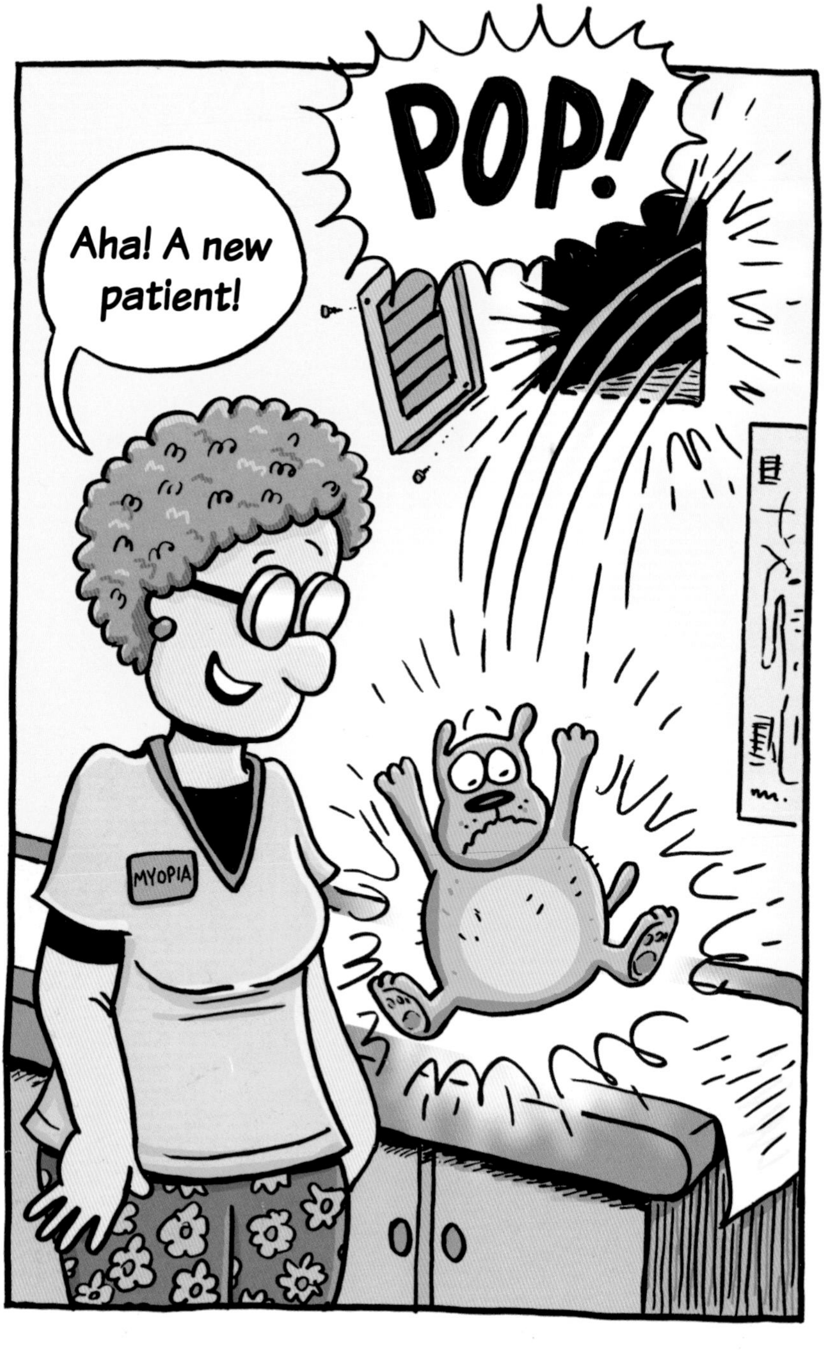
POP!
Aha! A new patient!
MYOPIA

Chubbs shot out of the vent and into the arms of a nearsighted back doctor.

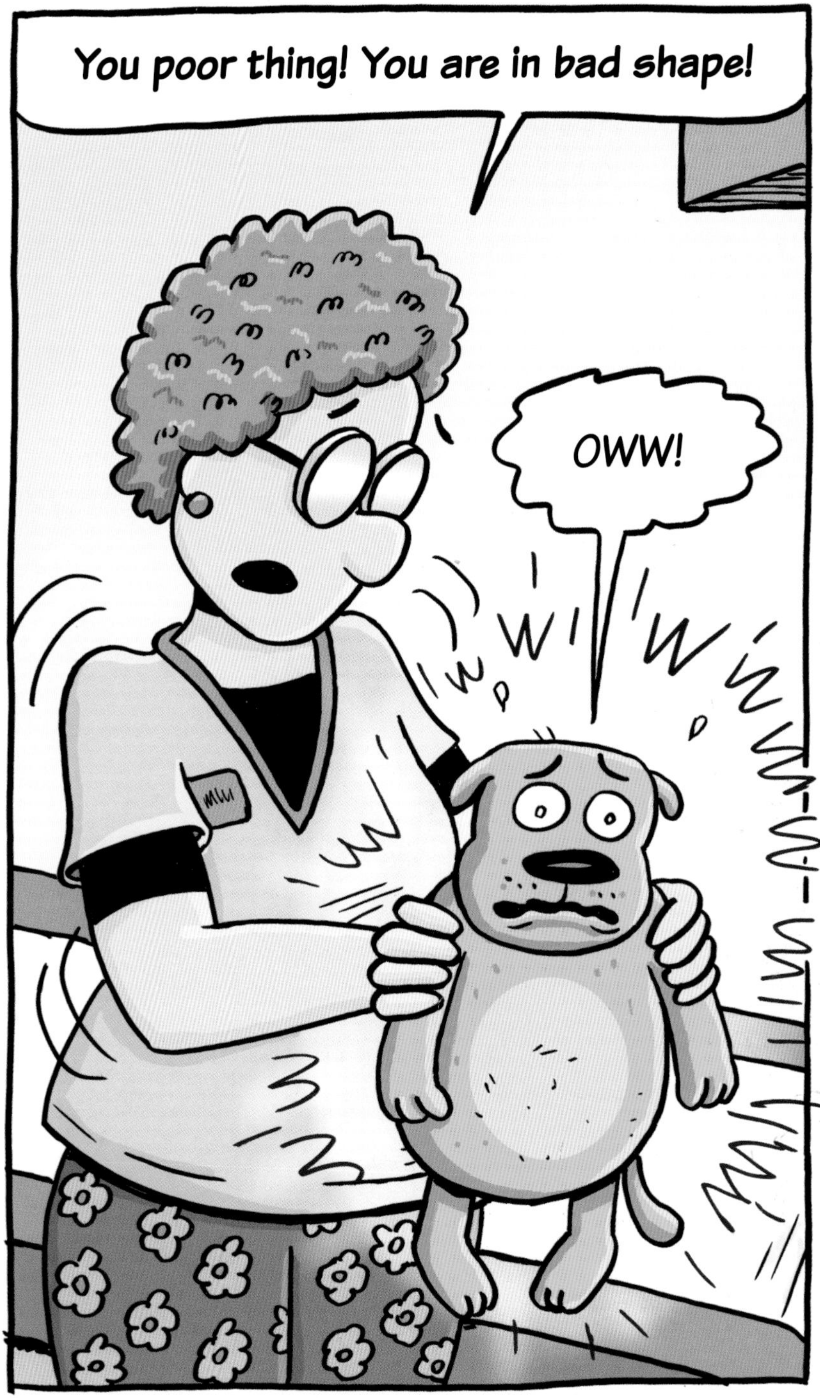
You poor thing! You are in bad shape!
OWW!

The city of El Dogrado was guarded by a six-armed beast that attacked poor Chubbs.

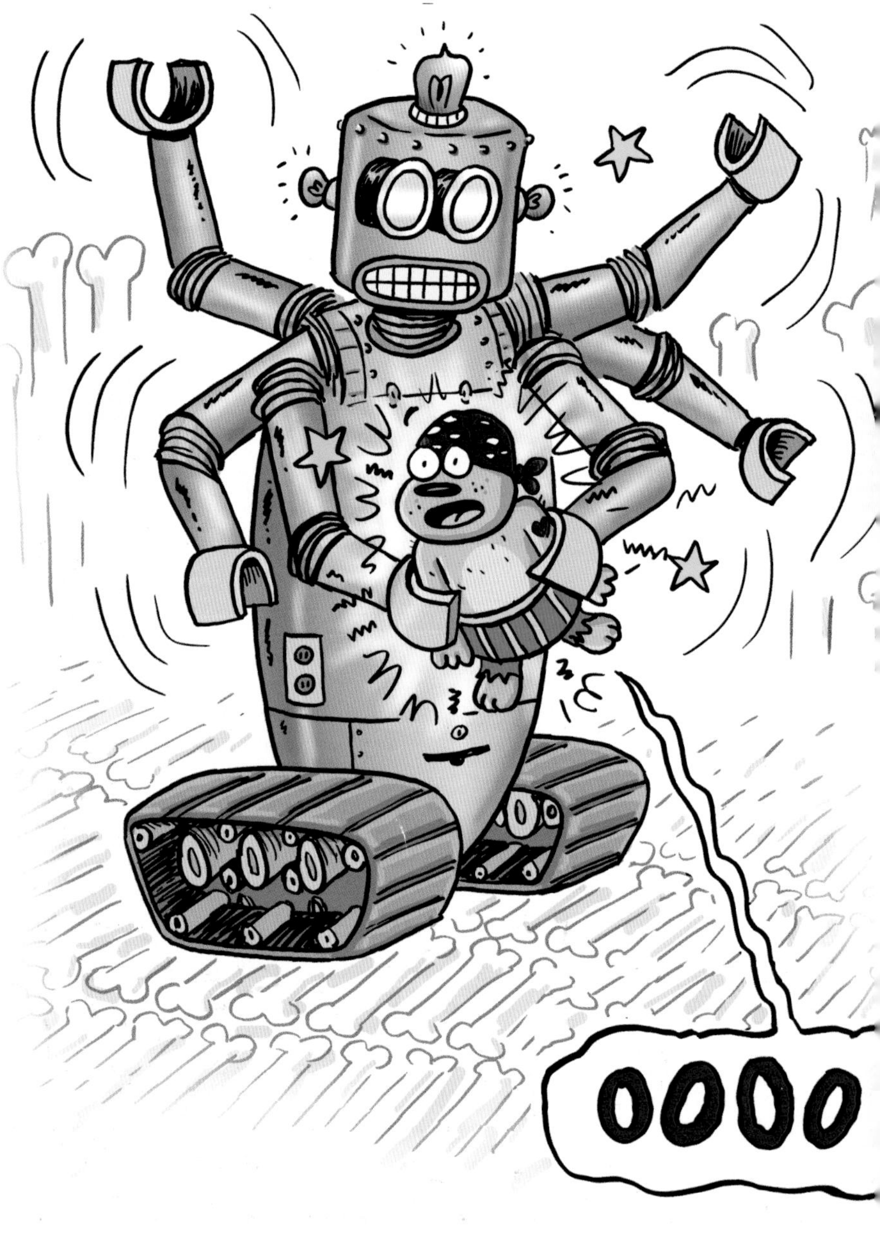
OOOO

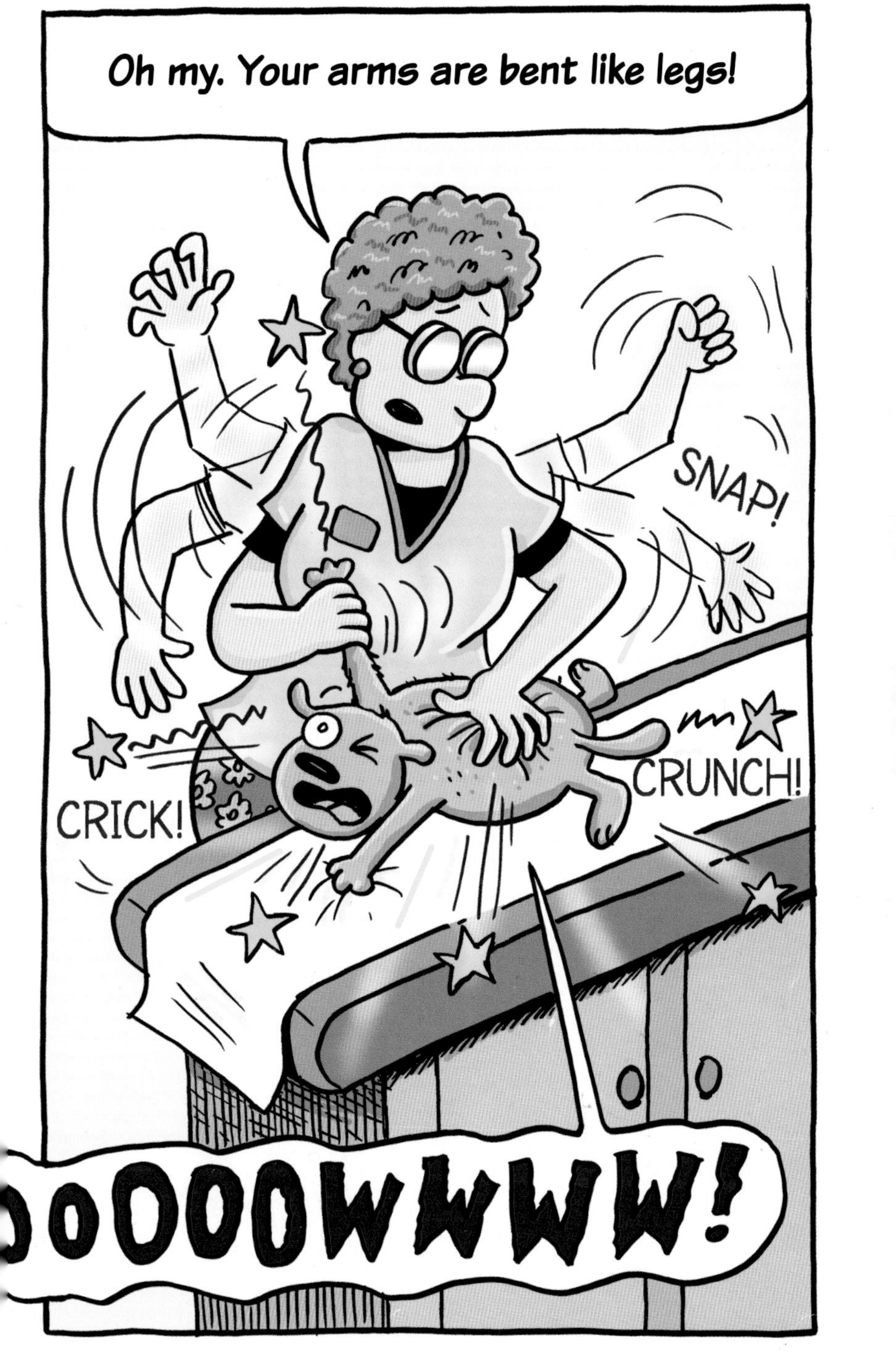
Oh my. Your arms are bent like legs!
SNAP!
CRICK!
CRUNCH!
OOOOOWWWWW!

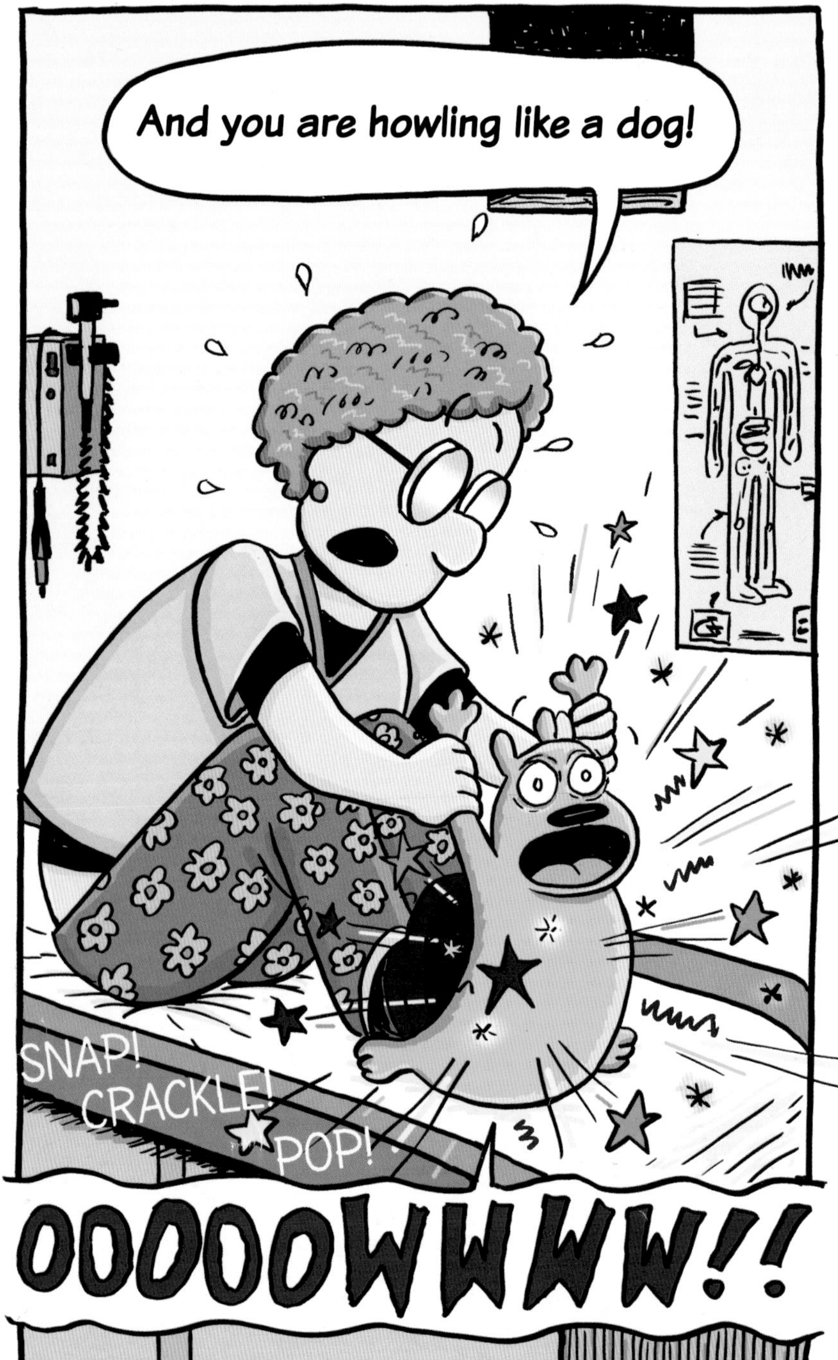
And you are howling like a dog!
SNAP!
CRACKLE!
POP!
OOOOOWWWW!!

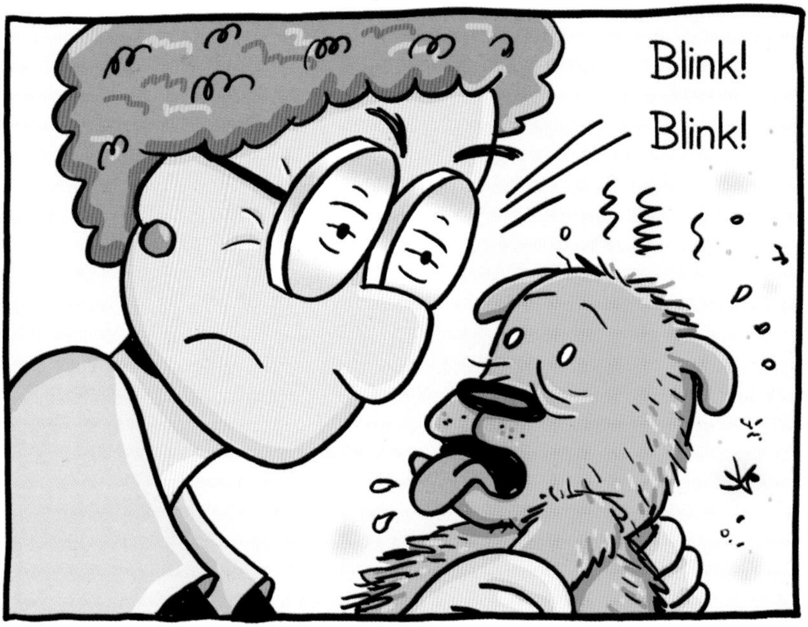
Blink!
Blink!

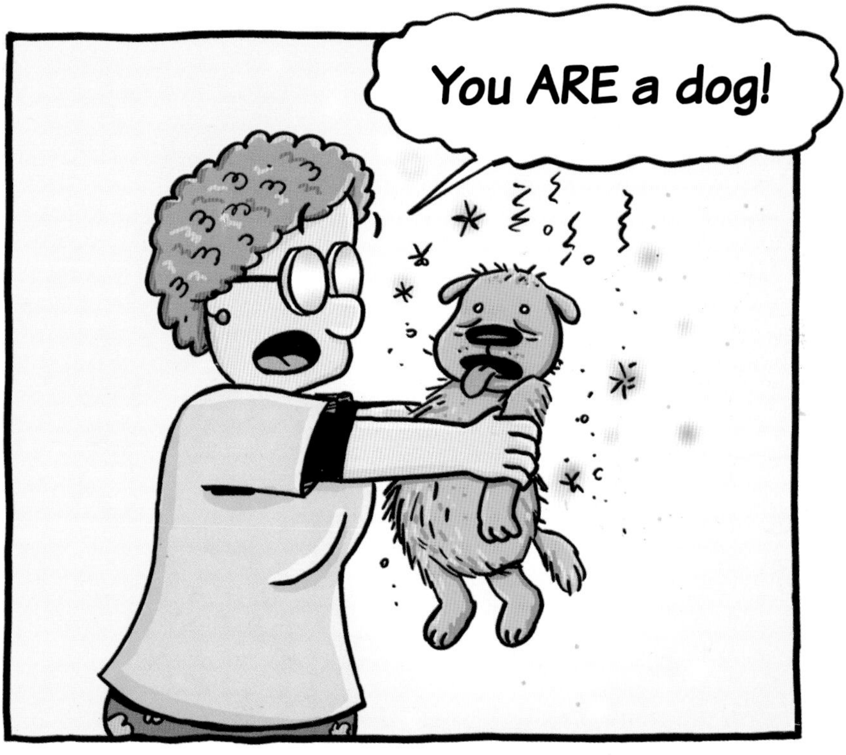
You ARE a dog!

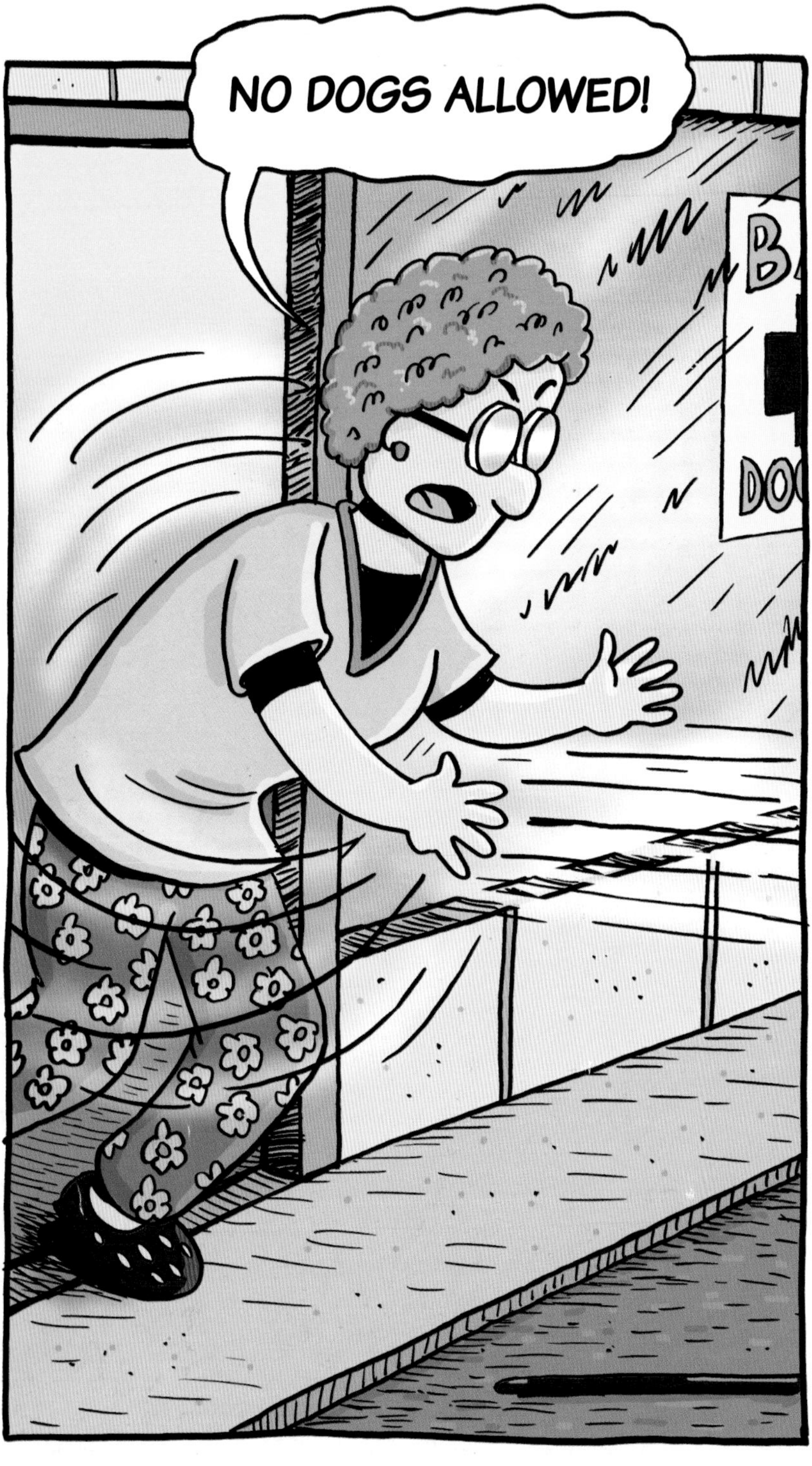
NO DOGS ALLOWED!

Chapter Seven

Chubbs was hurled out the door and crashed into the boat.

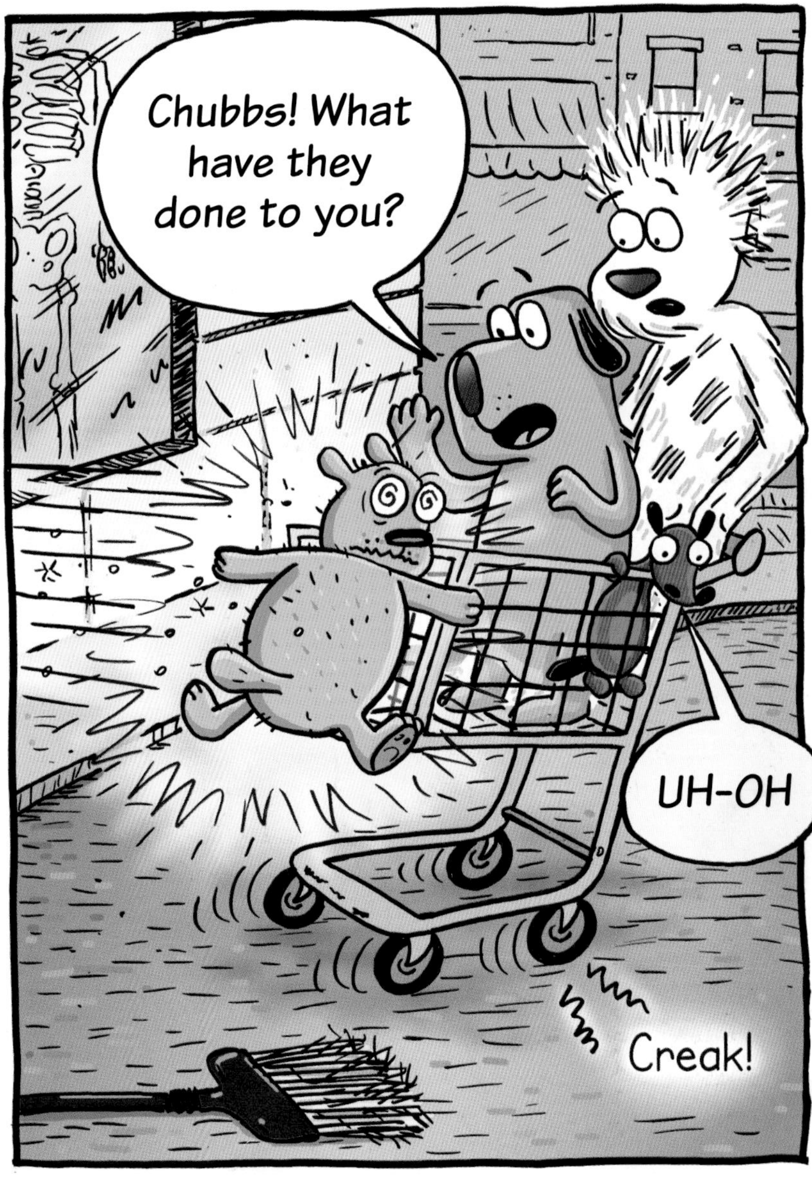
Chubbs! What have they done to you?
UH-OH
Creak!

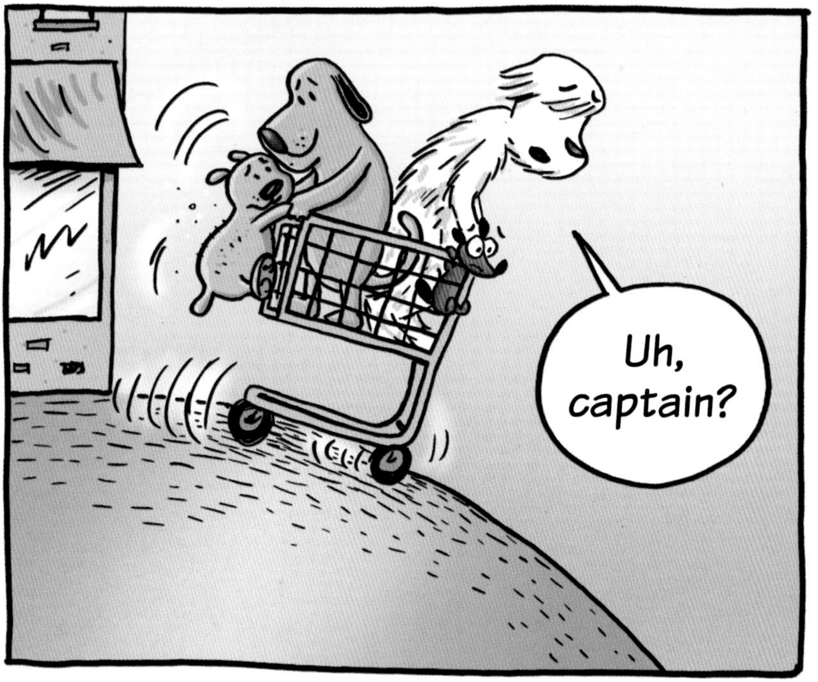
Uh, captain?

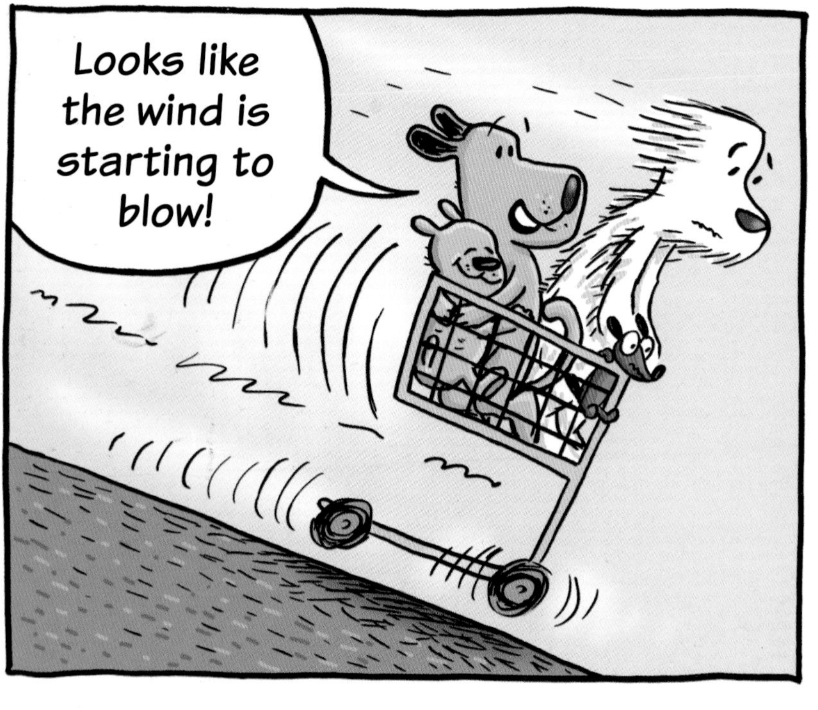
Looks like the wind is starting to blow!

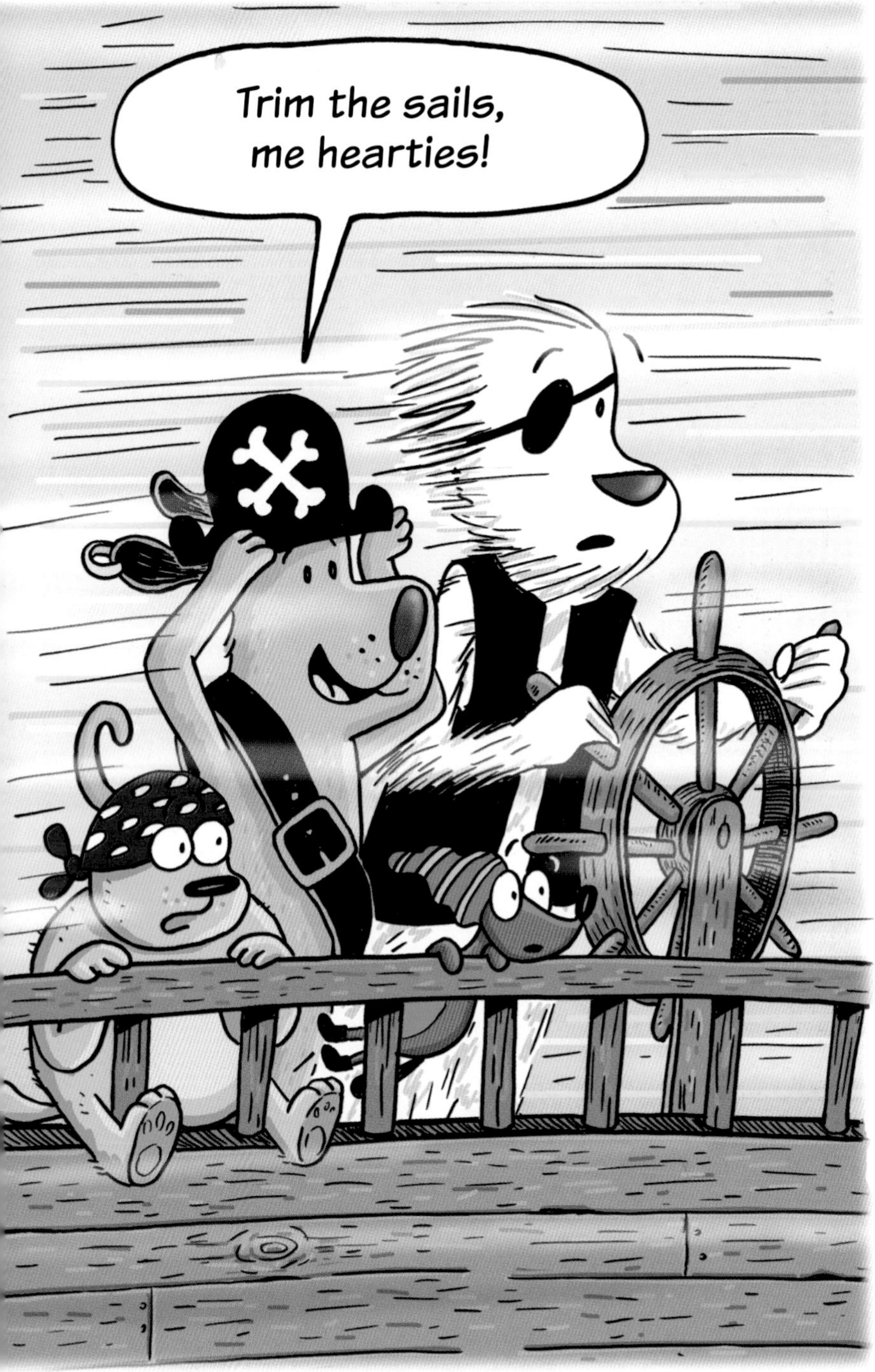
Trim the sails,
me hearties!

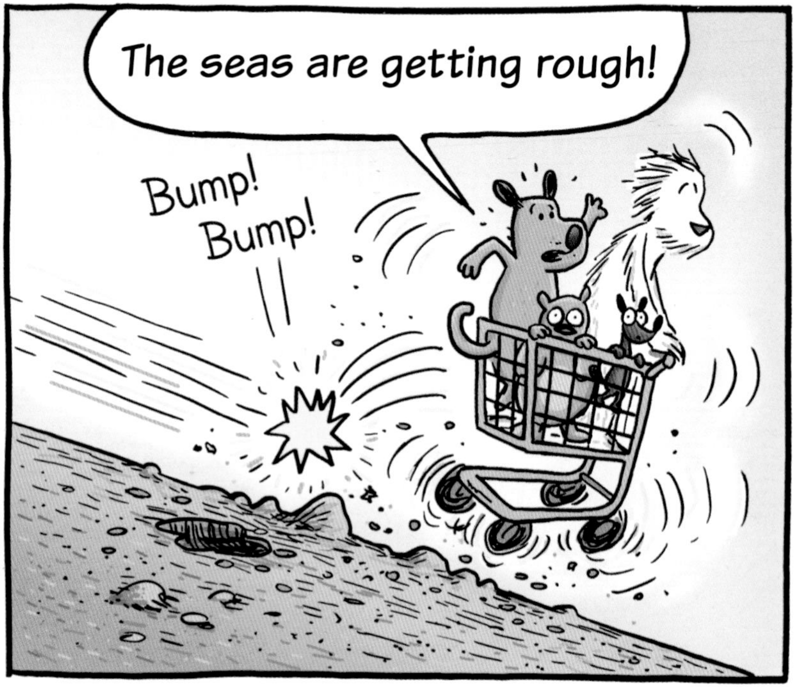
The seas are getting rough!
Bump! Bump!

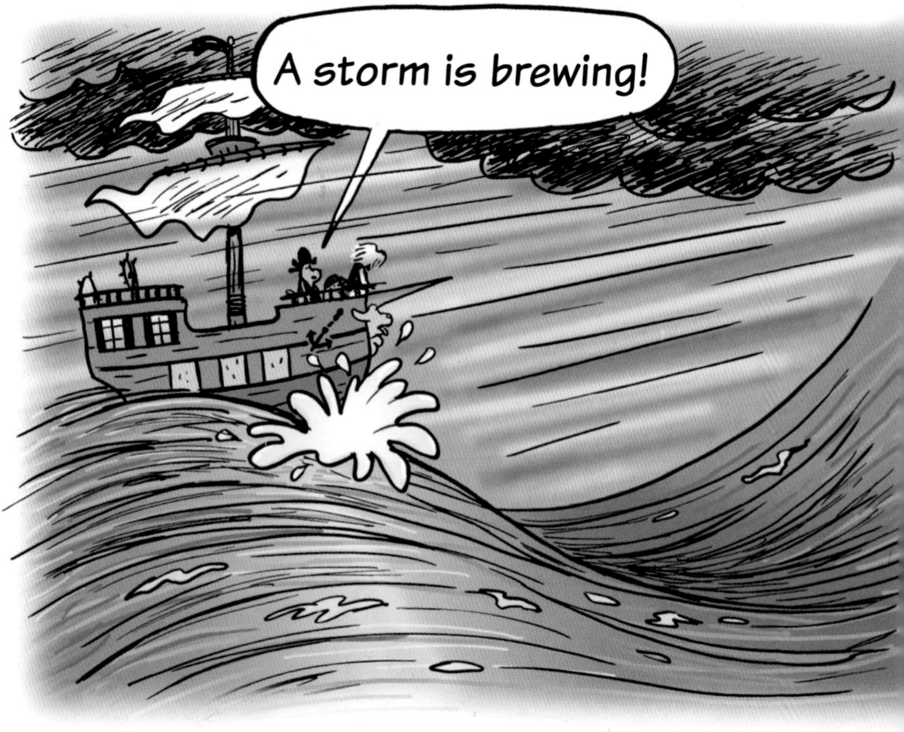
A storm is brewing!

Things did not look good for our brave pirates. So very brave.

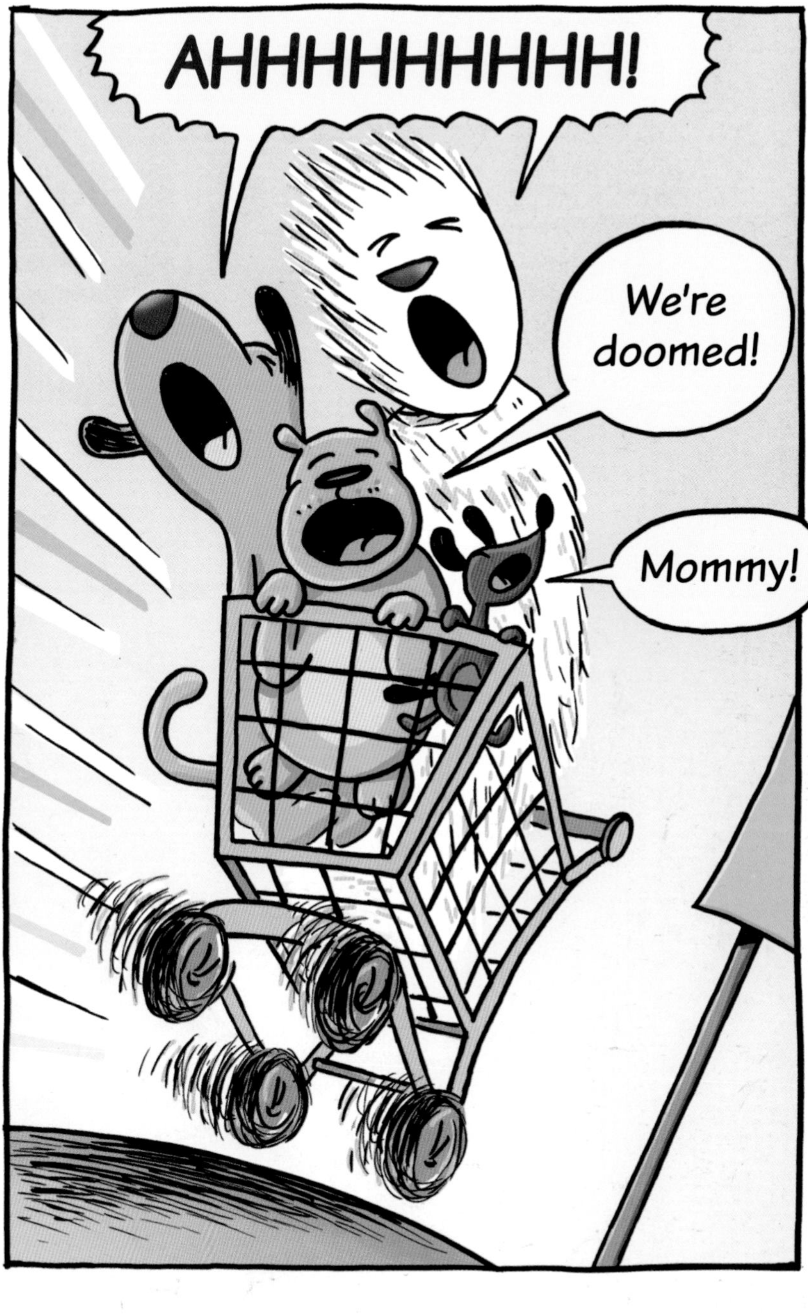
AHHHHHHHHHH!
We're doomed!
Mommy!

But then ...

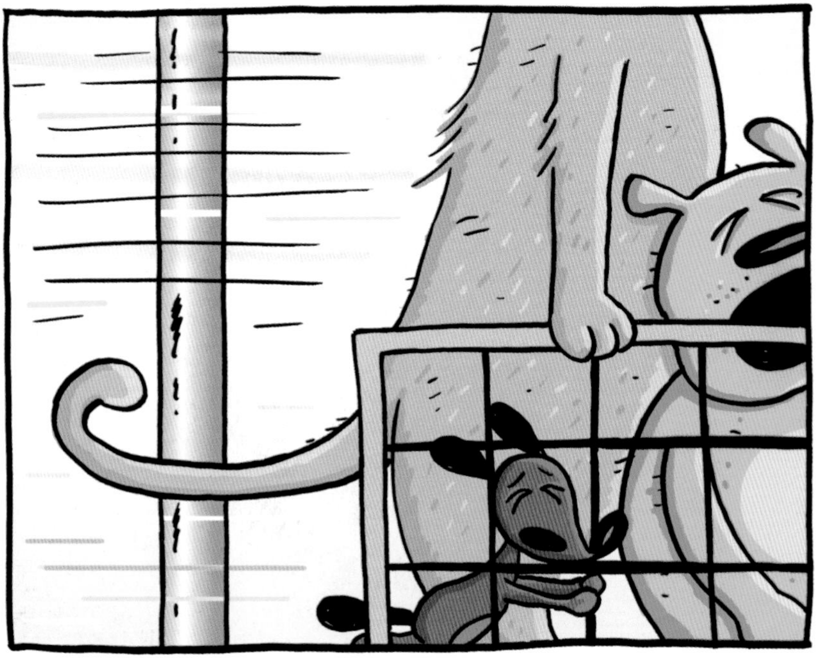

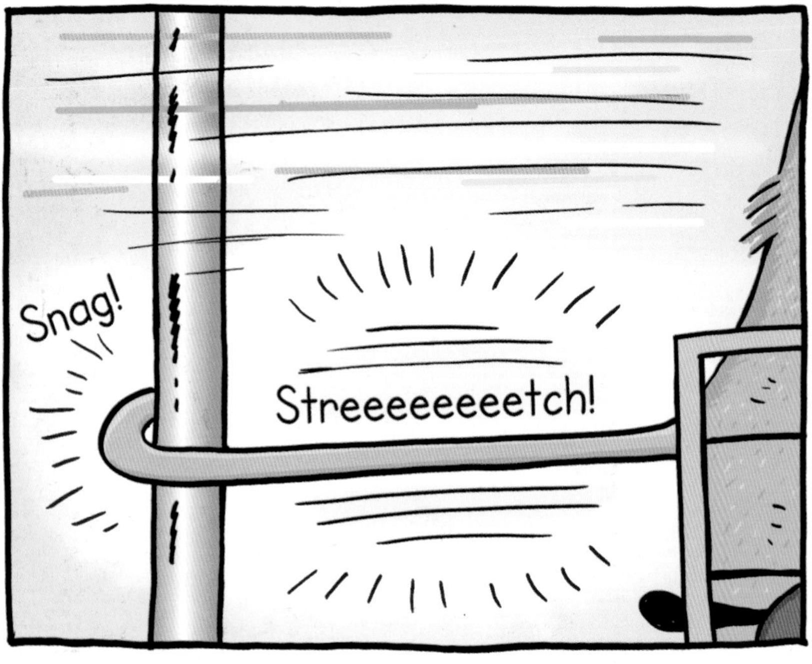
Snag!
Streeeeeeeetch!

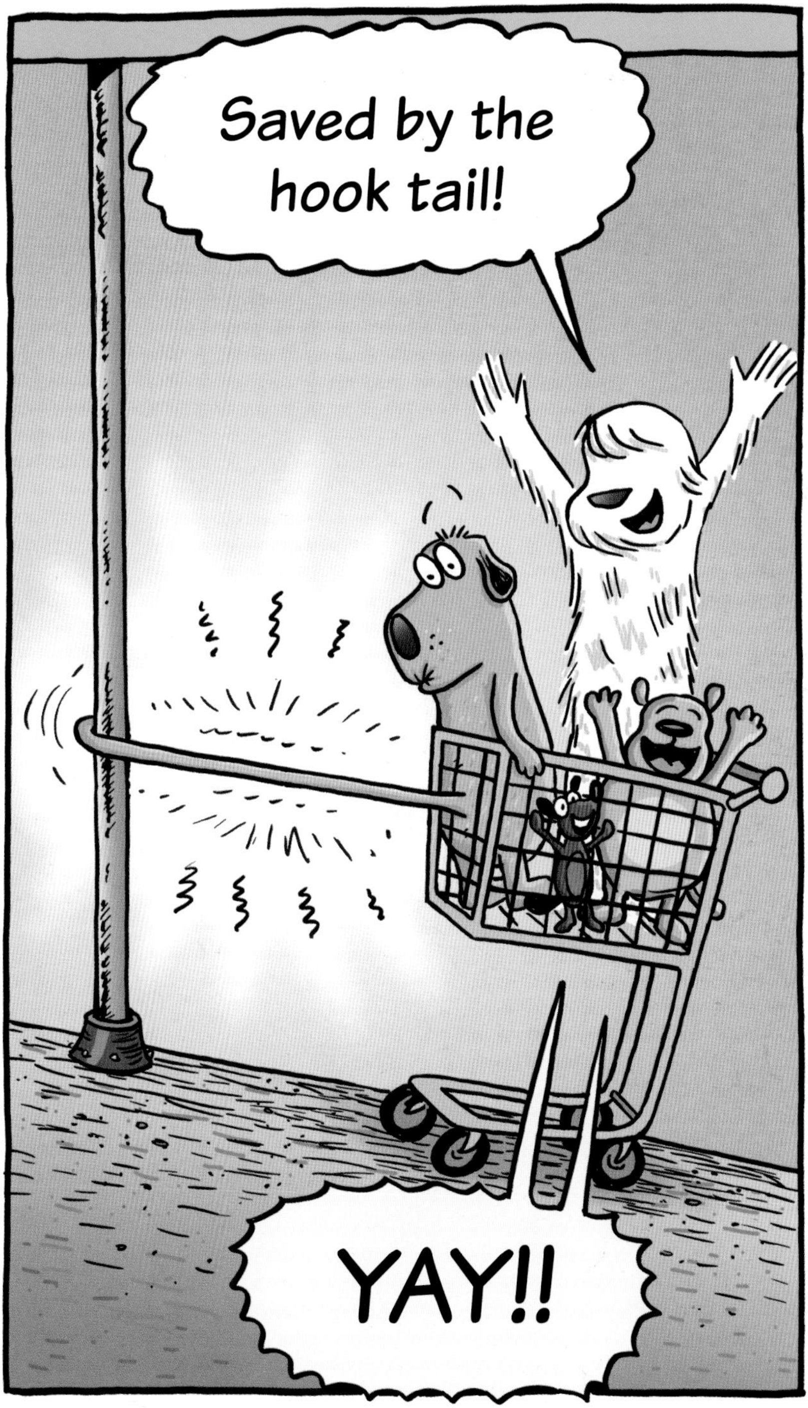
Saved by the hook tail!
YAY!!

Sadly, just when things were looking up, the captain looked up.

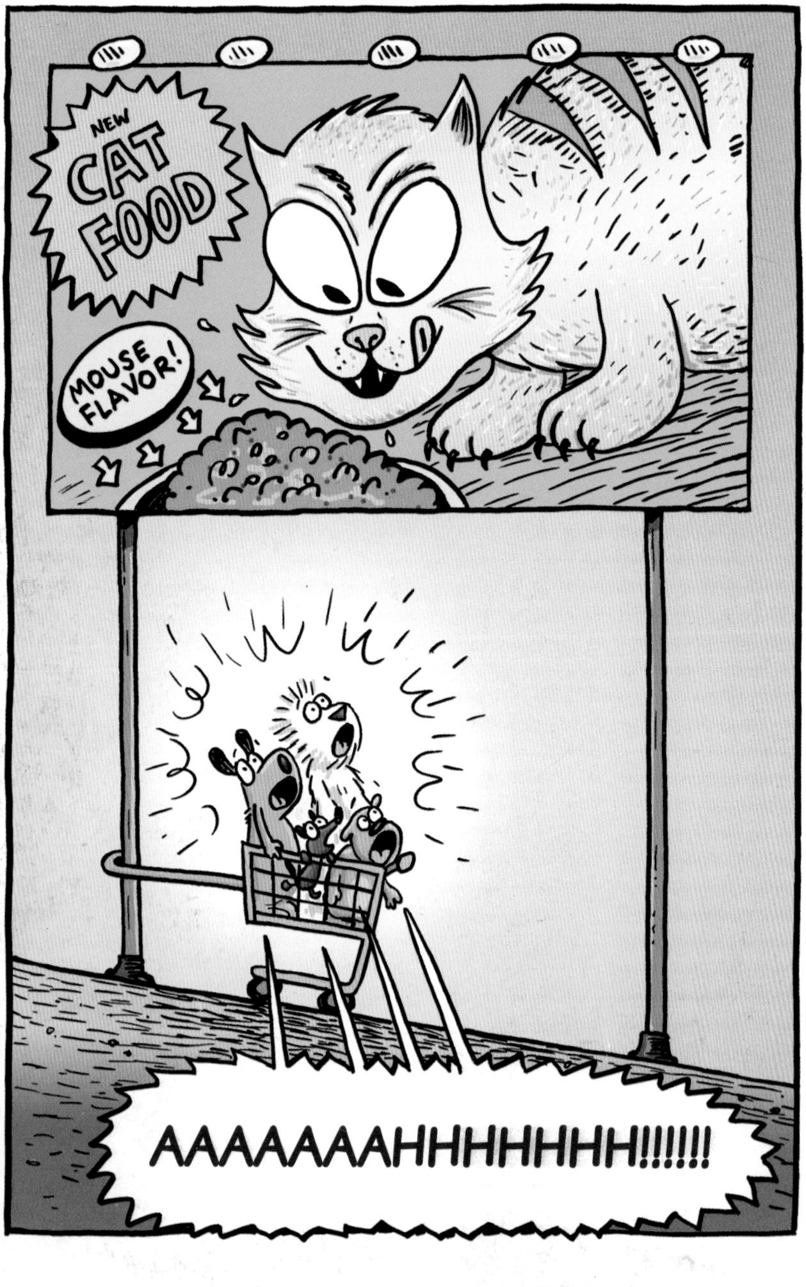
NEW
CAT FOOD
MOUSE FLAVOR!
AAAAAAAHHHHHHH!!!!!!

A giant sea-cat loomed over the ship!

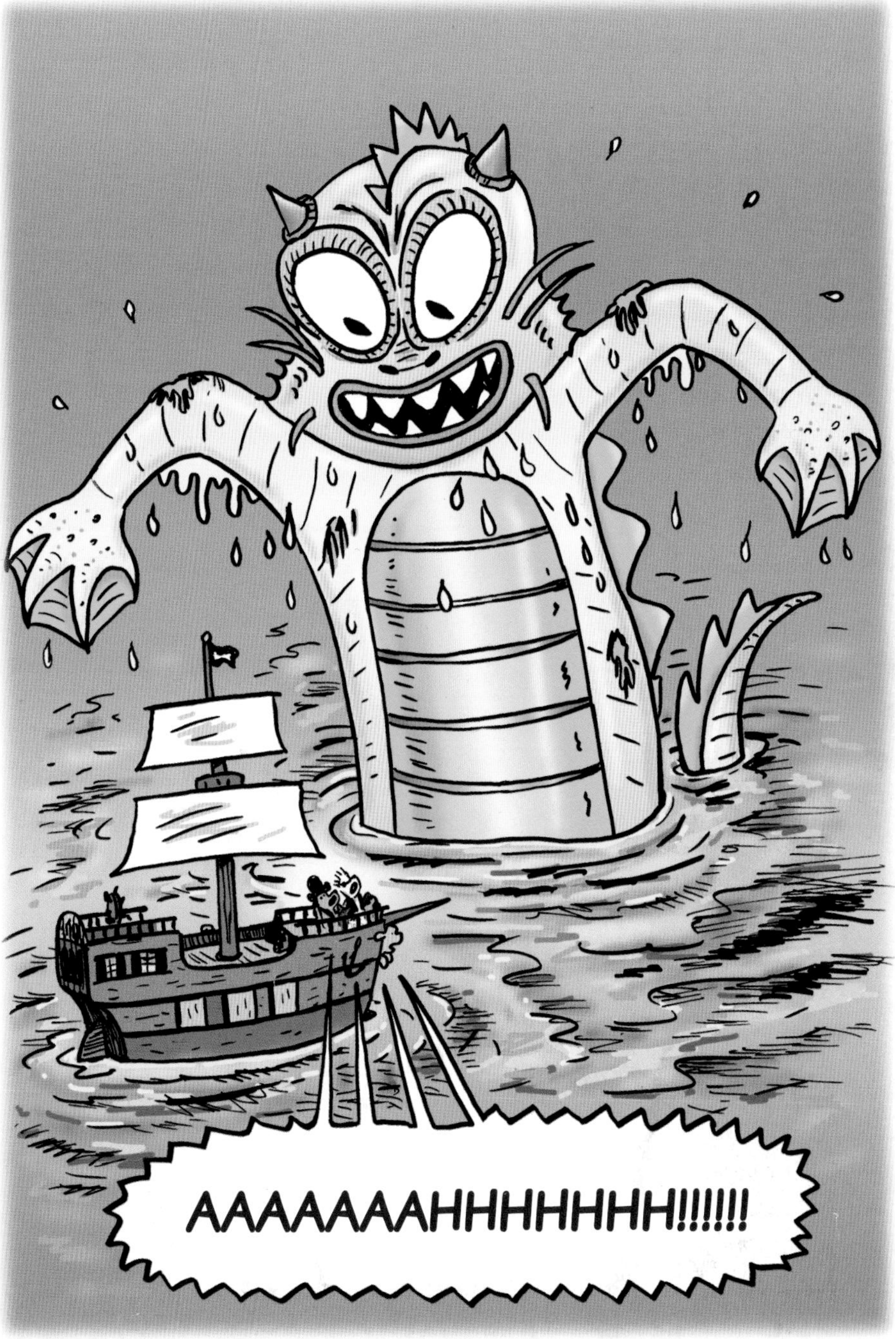
AAAAAAAHHHHHHH!!!!!!

Terror caused Captain Hooktail to lose his grip.

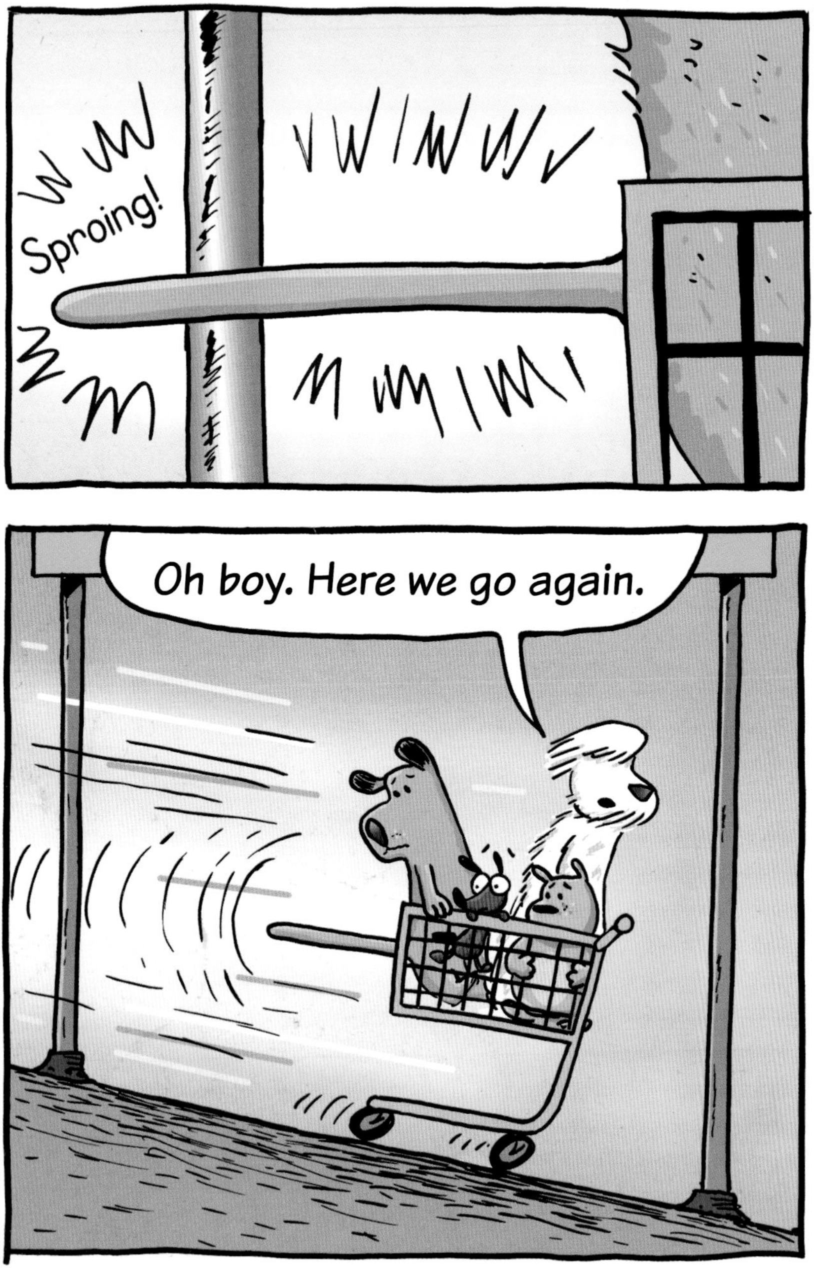
Sproing!
Oh boy. Here we go again.

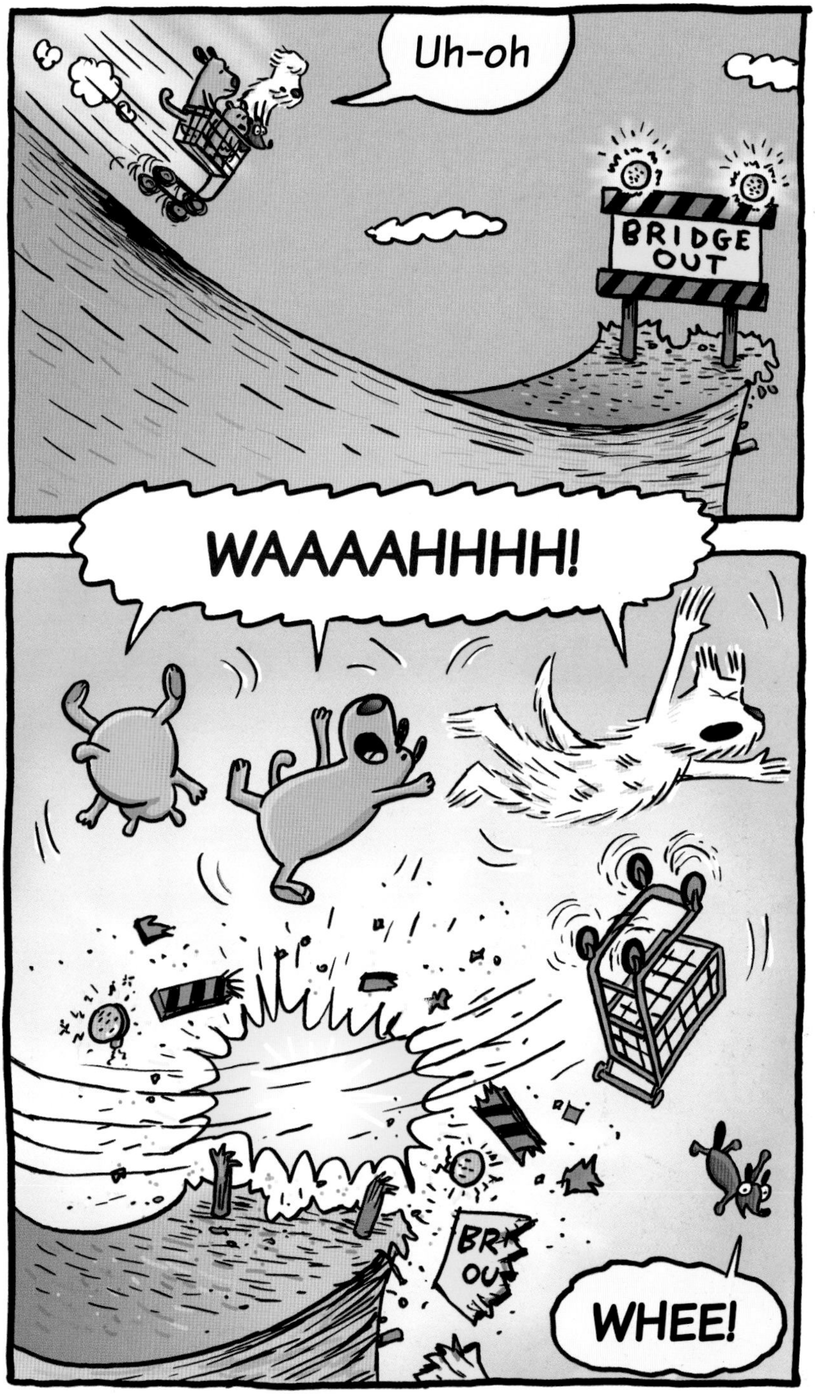
Uh-oh
BRIDGE OUT
WAAAAHHHH!
BR
OU
WHEE!

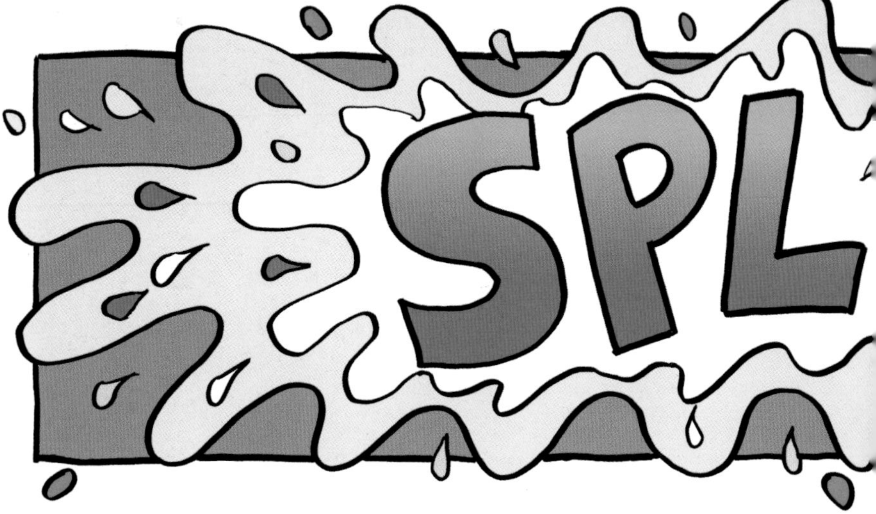
SPL

The HMS Beagle was sinking, so the Scurvy Dogs abandoned ship.

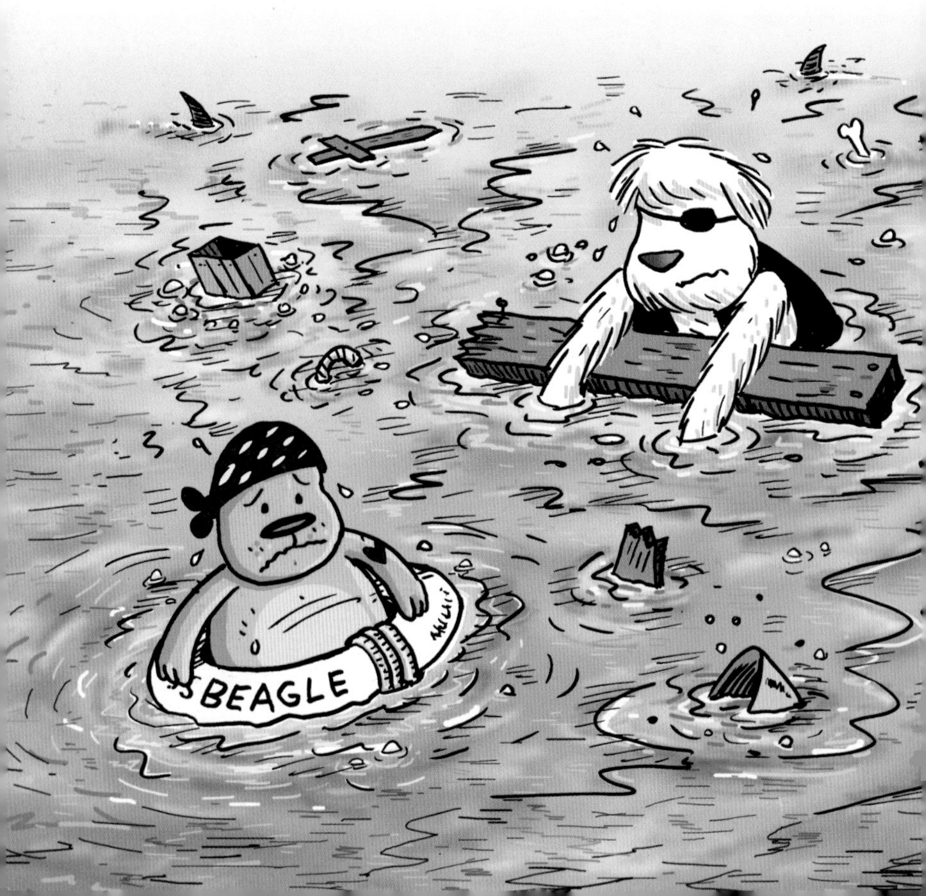
BEAGLE

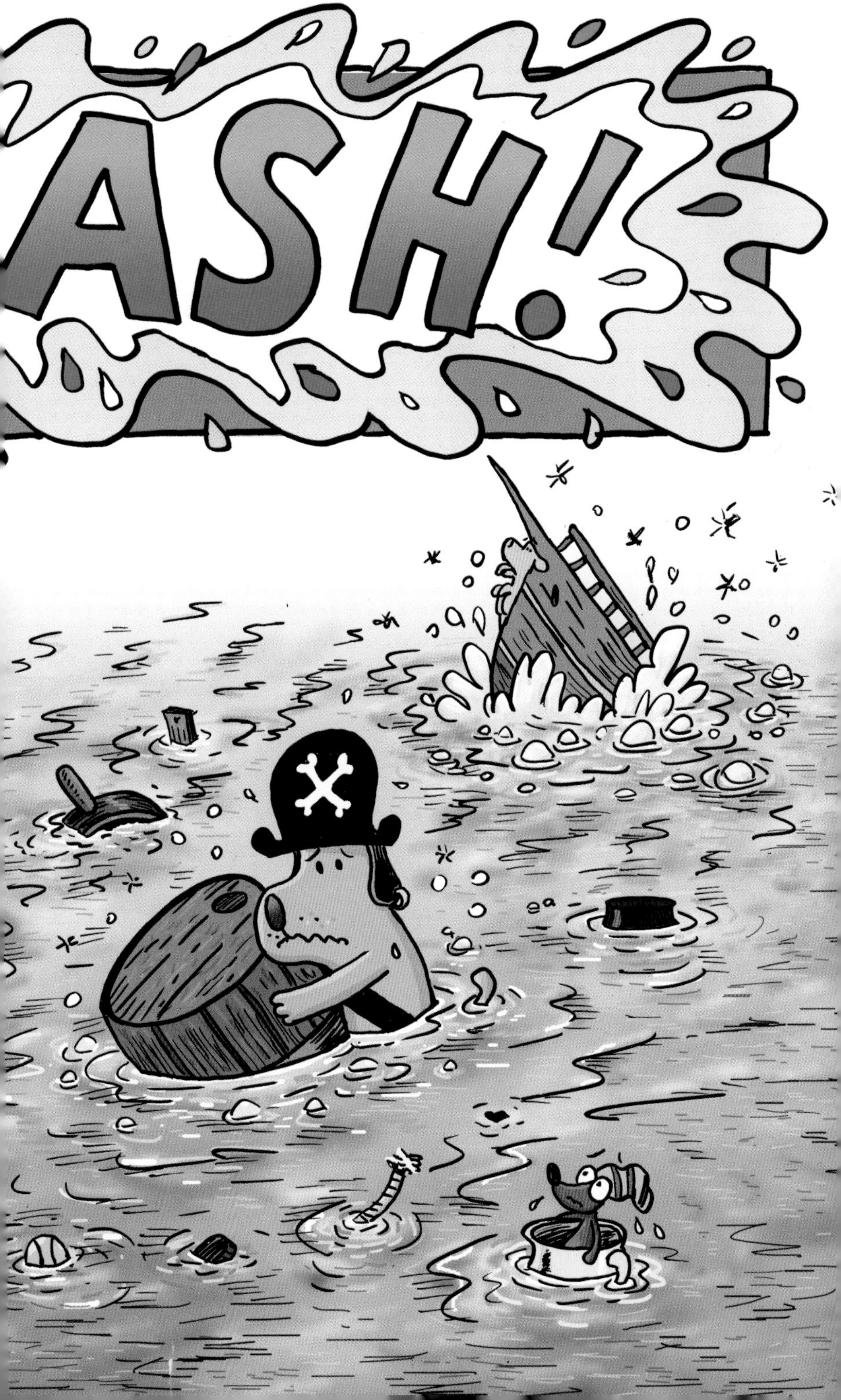
ASH!

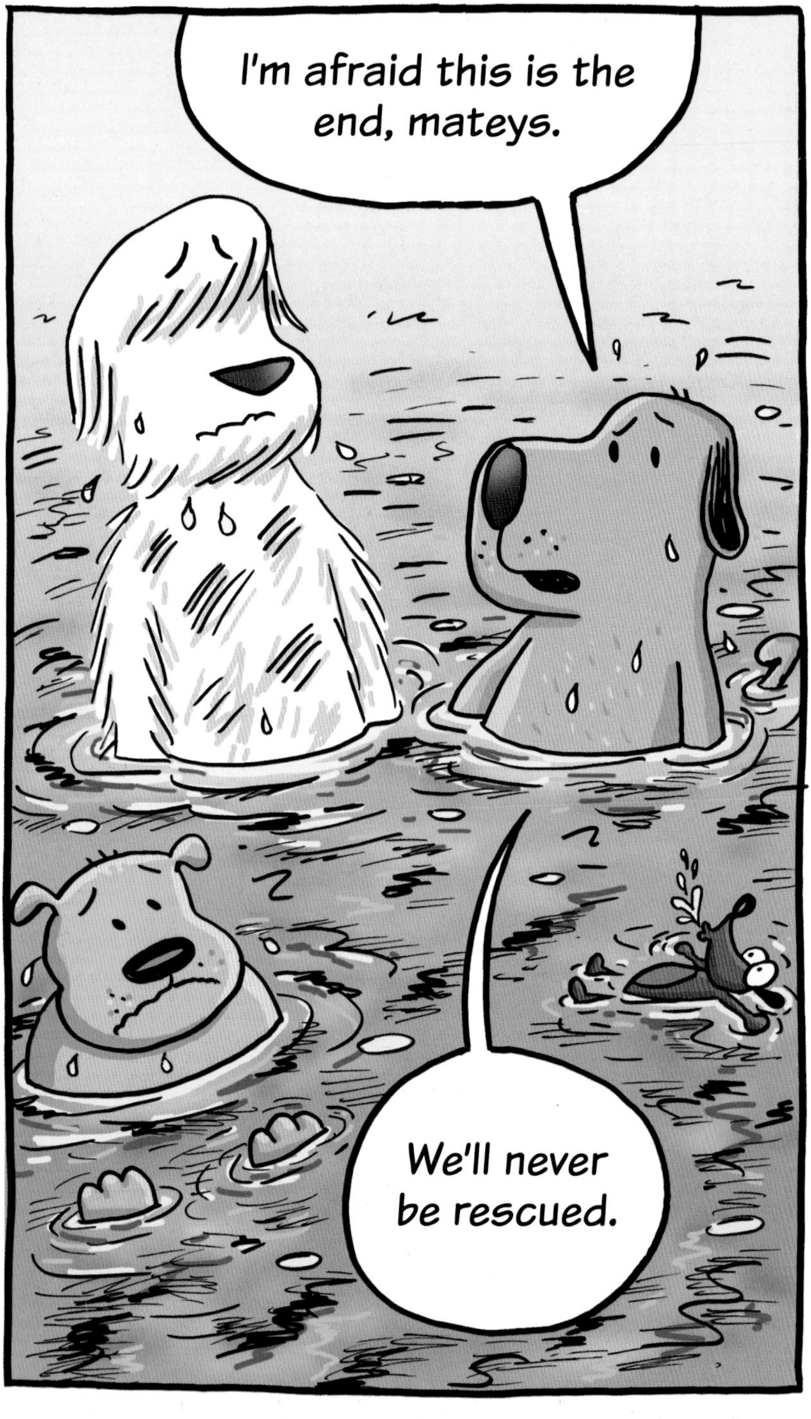

I'm afraid this is the end, mateys.
We'll never be rescued.

Chapter Eight

All seemed lost. But suddenly, a rescue ship appeared on the horizon, and a voice called out.

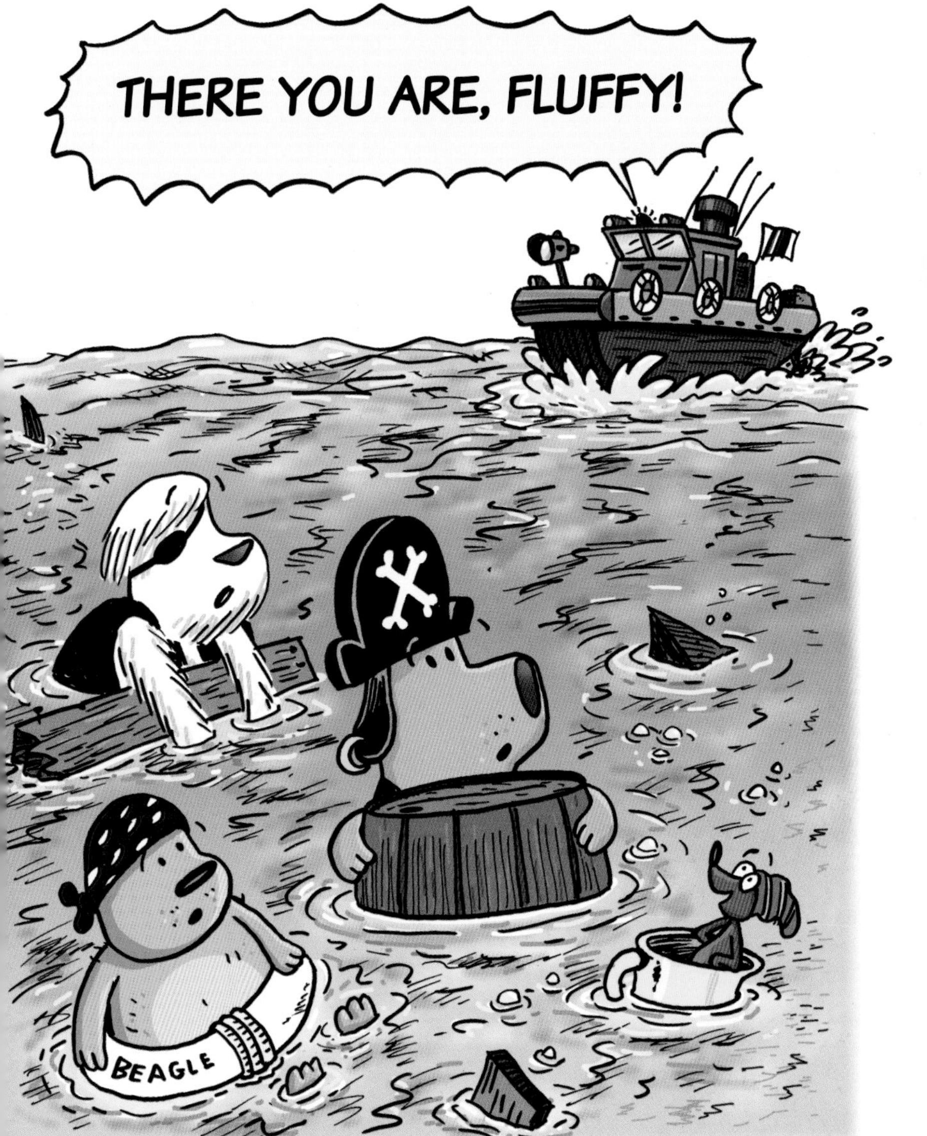
THERE YOU ARE, FLUFFY!
BEAGLE

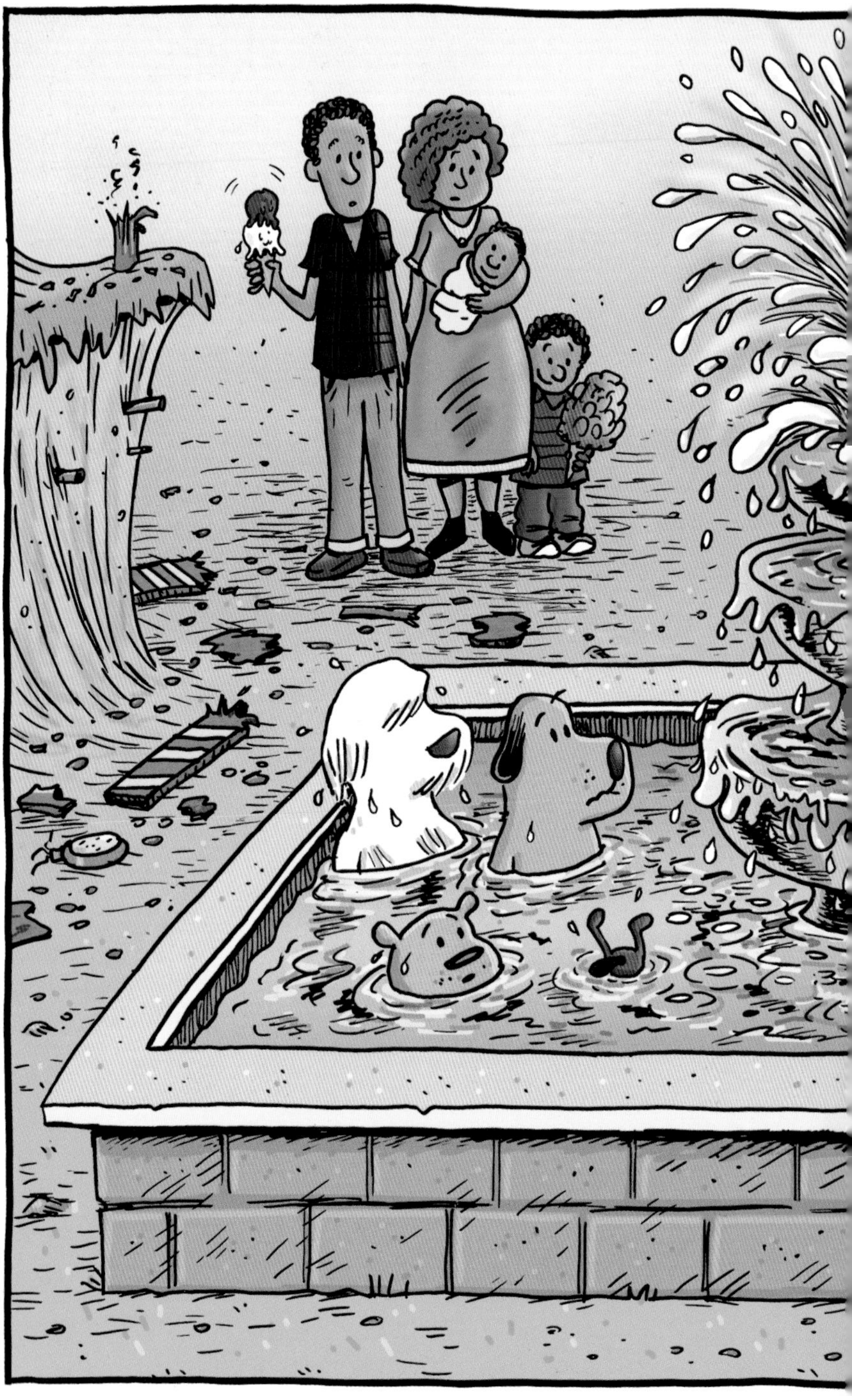

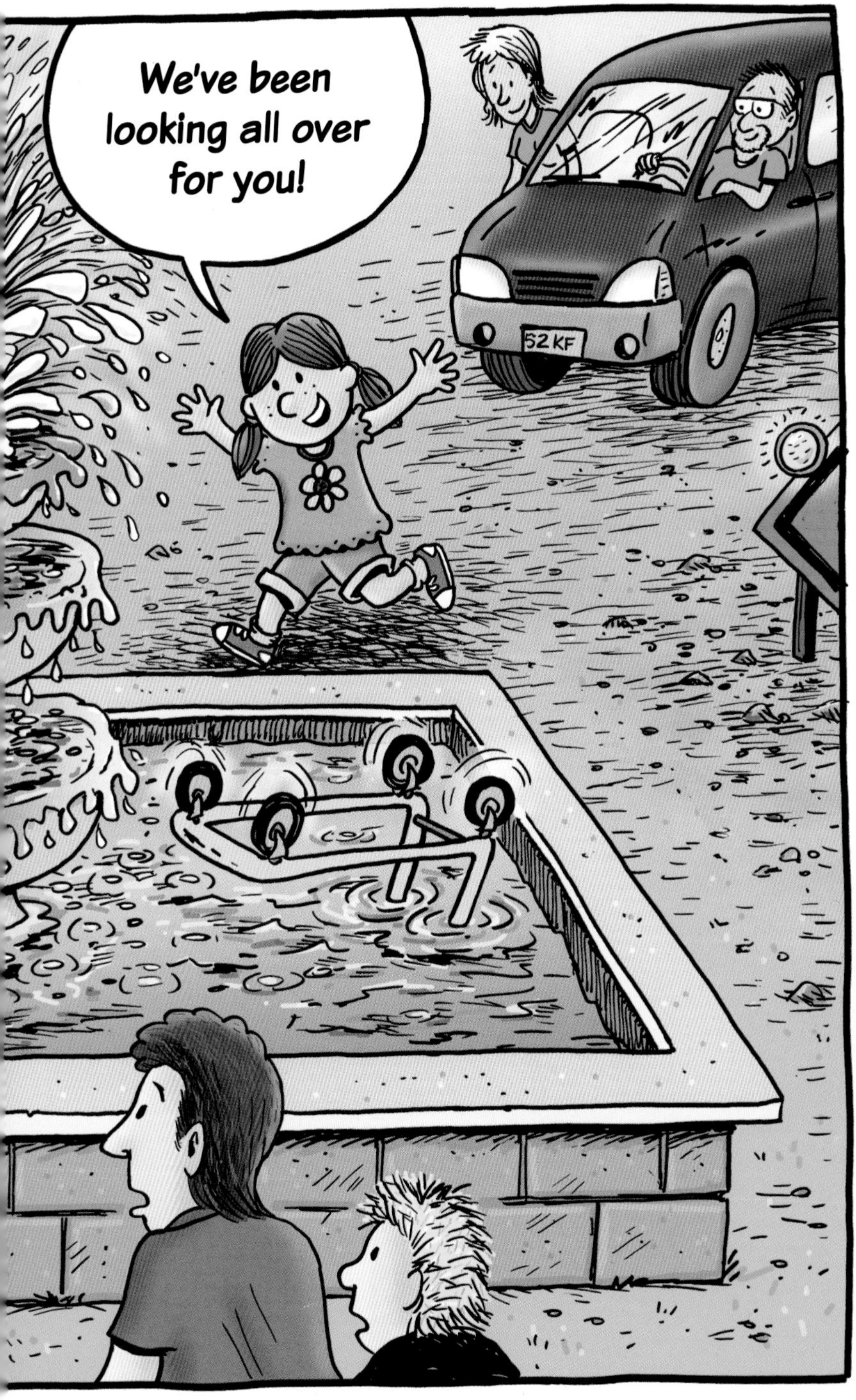
We've been looking all over for you!
52 KF

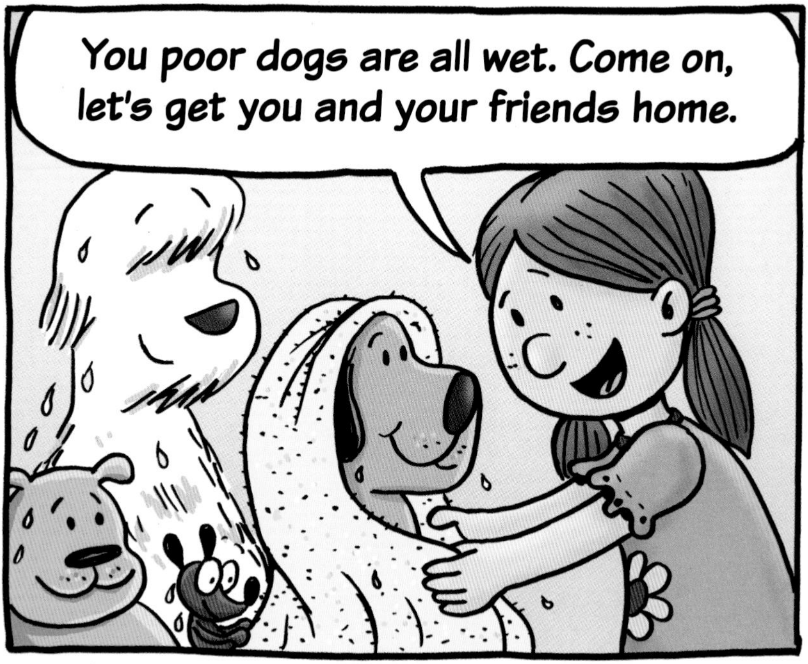
You poor dogs are all wet. Come on, let's get you and your friends home.

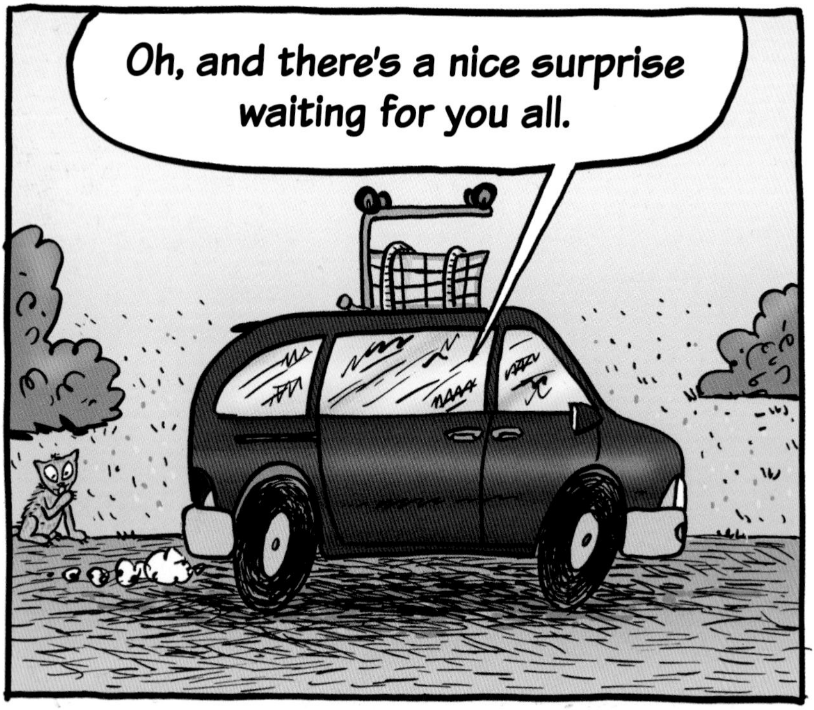
Oh, and there's a nice surprise waiting for you all.

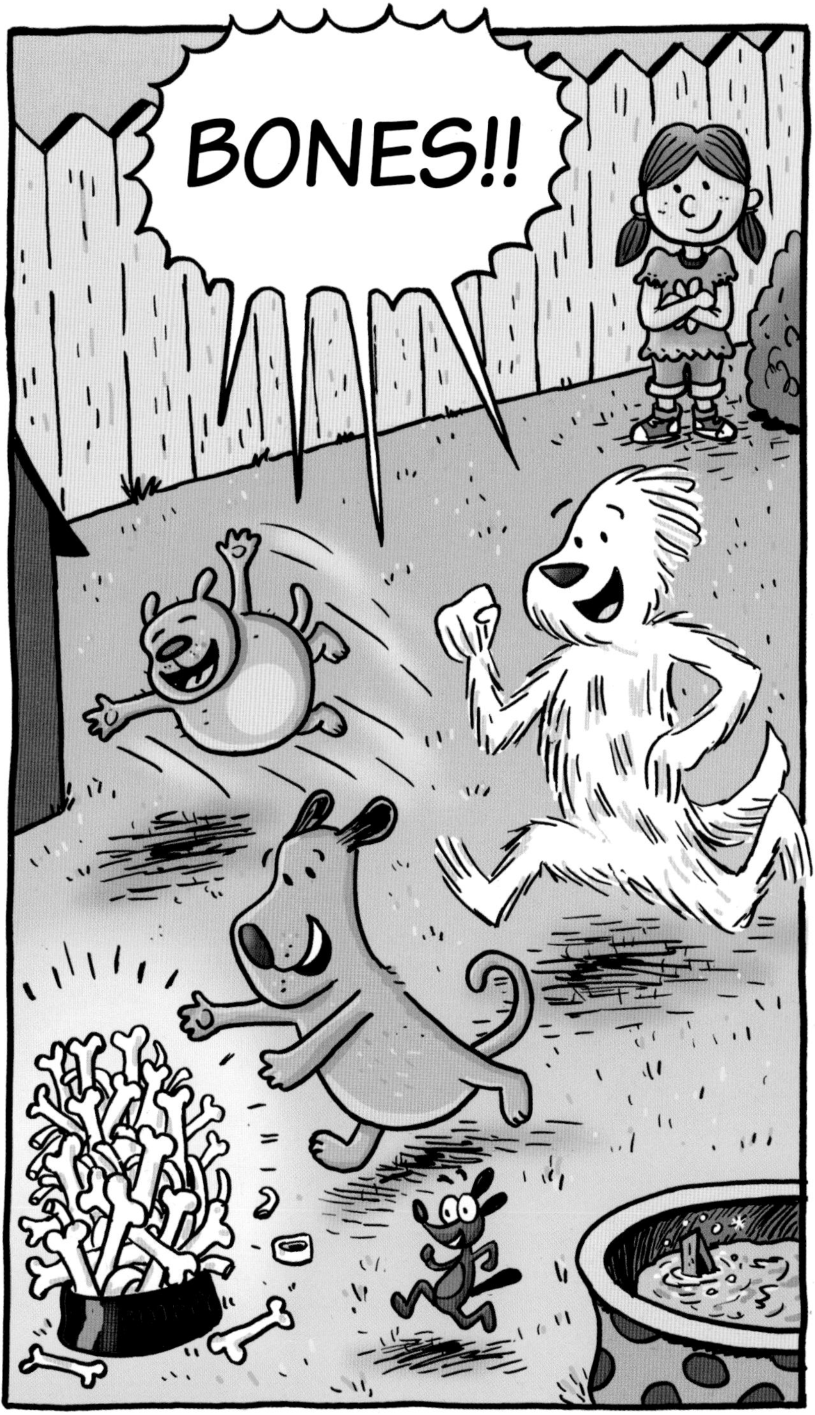
BONES!!

Their pirate ship was loaded with treasure, and so the victorious Scurvy Dogs sailed into the sunset.

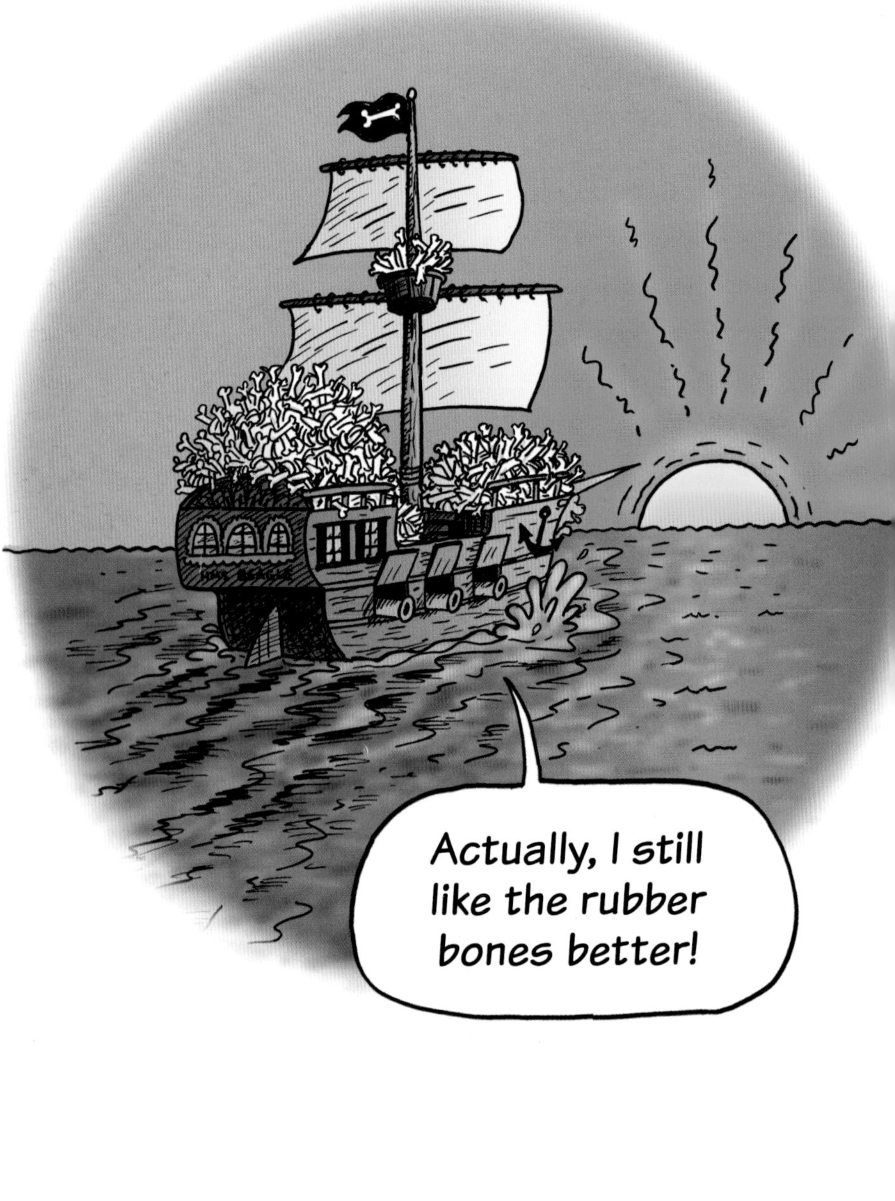
Actually, I still like the rubber bones better!

About the author

Kevin Frank is a multiple award-winning, internationally-syndicated cartoonist and illustrator. Originally from Illinois, he now calls a small town in Canada home. He steals his best material from his wife and three children. Visit him at www.kevinfrank.net